"Let's make the most of the time we have together now."

Sandra looked into Adam's eyes, feeling the familiar surge of arousal he so often called forth. He fascinated her, frustrated and confused her. He couldn't be good for her, but she couldn't stay away from him.

As he pulled her into the welcoming shadows, she draped herself around him, her lips locked to his in a kiss that made her forget everything short of her own name. Adam's hands slid down her back to cradle her bottom, and he pulled her closer still.

"Let's go to your yacht, where we can be alone," she said in a voice made low, husky by his kisses.

Without a word he took her hand and led her down the beach to explore a different world— one of shadows and secrets and sex....

Blaze™

Dear Reader,

I had so much fun on Passionata's Island with the characters in *At Her Pleasure* that I couldn't wait to revisit the island in this book. There's just something about sun, sand, sex—and pirates!

As part of my research for this book, I visited the *Titanic* exhibit that has been touring throughout the United States. One section of this exhibit was devoted to the process of locating and salvaging the ship's wreckage. I was amazed at the hard work that went into recovering and preserving artifacts. And several years ago I was lucky enough to tour an exhibition devoted to the pirate ship *Whydah*, a wooden sailing vessel much like the one I imagined for Passionata. Both of these exhibits, I hope, helped me bring my own shipwreck to life.

Many thanks also to my friend and fellow author Emily McKay, who helped me with my many questions about diving. Any mistakes in this book are mine, not hers.

Of course, once all the research was done, it was time to put my imagination to work. That's where the real fun began. I hope you'll enjoy Adam and Sandra's story as much as I did. Let me know what you think by e-mailing me at cindi@cindimyers.com, or write to me in care of Harlequin Enterprises, 225 Duncan Mill Rd, Toronto, Ontario, M3B 3K9, Canada.

Cindi Myers

HER SECRET TREASURE
Cindi Myers

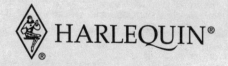

HARLEQUIN®

TORONTO • NEW YORK • LONDON
AMSTERDAM • PARIS • SYDNEY • HAMBURG
STOCKHOLM • ATHENS • TOKYO • MILAN • MADRID
PRAGUE • WARSAW • BUDAPEST • AUCKLAND

ISBN-13: 978-0-373-79431-7
ISBN-10:   0-373-79431-2

HER SECRET TREASURE

This edition published by arrangement with Harlequin Books S.A.

® and TM are trademarks of the publisher. Trademarks indicated with ® are registered in the United States Patent and Trademark Office, the Canadian Trade Marks Office and in other countries.

www.eHarlequin.com

Printed in U.S.A.

ABOUT THE AUTHOR

Cindi Myers's dreams of sailing away to an island paradise with her own swashbuckling pirate have been quashed by rampant seasickness and a tendency to sunburn easily. So she settles for drinking umbrella cocktails and letting her imagination run wild on the sun-washed beaches of her books.

Books by Cindi Myers

Don't miss any of our special offers. Write to us at the following address for information on our newest releases.

Harlequin Reader Service
U.S.: 3010 Walden Ave., P.O. Box 1325, Buffalo, NY 14269
Canadian: P.O. Box 609, Fort Erie, Ont. L2A 5X3

This one's for Tammy

1

THE DREAMS HAD BEGUN on her first visit to the island—strange nighttime fantasies she could never clearly recall, which left her confused and strangely aroused. Sandra Newman was not a person who indulged in superstition or whimsy, but those island dreams haunted her, leaving her with the sense that understanding them would reveal the secret to unfulfilled longings she hadn't realized she possessed.

The memory of those dreams was with her now, as her yacht sailed within sight of the palm-covered atoll. Passionata's Island was named after the female pirate who had headquartered there in the early days of the eighteenth century, a pirate queen known for her successful attacks on merchant ships that ventured too near her sanctuary, and acclaimed for her skill as a seductress.

"Jonas, I want a good shot of the island as we approach," she directed her cameraman, who obligingly aimed his handheld video camera over the ship's bow. "I'm thinking this is our opening," she continued. "Maybe with some mysterious music and a voice-over talking about the reputed curse on the island." Oh, yes, this place even had a curse. Talk about a made-for-television story. Passionata was a tragic-romantic figure who had left behind treasure worth millions—perhaps even billions—of dollars. She smiled, imagining the network head, Gary Simon's eyes popping when he saw the numbers for audience share when *Sandra Newman Presents Passionata's Treasure,* aired next fall. He'd be tripping all over himself to offer her a new, more-lucrative contract.

As the yacht rounded the reef at one end of the island and headed toward the deeper harbor on the west side, two other vessels already anchored there caught Sandra's attention. The larger one, the *Caspian,* was unfamiliar to her. The ship bristled with cranes, lifts and a flotilla of smaller dinghies and motorboats.

The smaller ship was anchored nearer the island—a graceful sailing yacht with a white hull and gleaming teak deck. The sight of it made Sandra's pulse race a little faster.

Right on cue, a burly blonde dressed in nothing but faded blue swim trunks emerged from the cabin to watch her approach. She couldn't decide if she was glad to see that Professor Adam Carroway had arrived safely, or annoyed that she was going to spend the next few months in close proximity to the aggravating academic. The memory of the intense yet brief affair they'd enjoyed months ago added to her ambivalence about him.

Adam was a single-minded professor who focused on his quest for the *Eve,* Passionata's flagship that had sunk in 1714. While he was working, he neglected everything else, even forgetting to eat, and wearing the same worn clothes for days at a time. He was also a supremely masculine, energetic lover, very different from the smooth, sophisticated men she preferred. So why did she find Adam Carroway so…distracting? For whatever reason, the scruffy professor stirred something in her. She'd enjoyed the few days—and nights— they'd spent together when he'd visited her in Los Angeles last year. They'd parted as friends, with no talk of the future. But now the future was here, and she wasn't sure how she felt about seeing him again. Yes, it might be fun to pick up where they left off and enjoy a summer fling. Yet Adam' had a way of getting to her that no other man had. She'd never admit that to him, but maybe it would be better in the long run to keep things strictly business between them. Allowing herself to be vulnerable had never brought her anything but trouble.

Twenty minutes later, when Sandra's yacht was safely anchored, Adam was climbing aboard. Still wearing only swim trunks and dark sunglasses, his blond hair tangled by the wind, and several days' growth of beard fringing his chin, he could have been one of Passionata's contemporaries. The kind of man who was sure to thrill her television audience, Sandra reminded herself, ignoring the shiver of arousal that rushed through her at his approach.

"Hello, Sandra," he said, nodding by way of greeting. Despite the dark glasses, she could almost feel his gaze on her.

"And how are you, Professor?" She gave him her most charming smile. "The trip from Jamaica went smoothly. Thank you so much for asking."

He crossed his arms over his barrel chest, biceps bulging in a way she found unnervingly distracting. "Are you all set to begin filming?" he asked. "We're starting work first thing in the morning."

"I'm ready." She'd been waiting months for this chance to prove to the network that she was still a star.

"Remember, we have an agreement," Adam continued. "You and your crew will stay out of our way while we're working on the wreck. The last thing I need is to worry about one of you getting hurt."

She struck a seductive pose against the railing. "Why, Adam, I didn't know you cared."

His mouth twitched. She wished she could see his eyes, could read the expression there. Was he remembering those hot nights in L.A.? "I care about this salvage operation going as smoothly as possible," he said. "I don't want anything—or anyone—getting in my way."

Was this his way of telling her there'd be no resumption of their physical relationship? As if the decision was entirely up to him? She straightened and kept her voice even, her emotions in check. "I've paid a lot of money for the privilege of recording your every movement over the next few months," she said. "I'm every bit as invested in this operation running smoothly as you are."

She'd had to fight hard for the funding to make this trip, and she couldn't afford to return to the States empty-handed. Her last production had tanked in the ratings, through no fault of her own. The powers-that-be at the network had decided to air her show opposite the most hotly contested Super Bowl in two decades, then had the nerve to blame her for the failure to draw a big audience. They'd told her expensive documentaries were out of style now and had made clear that *Passionata's Treasure* was her last chance to prove herself.

That was nothing new, she reminded herself. She'd spent her career—her entire life, really—proving herself to those who underestimated her.

"Good." He turned and started toward the rail. "I'll see you later. I have work to do now."

"Adam, don't go." Maybe they wouldn't be lovers again, but she'd be damned if she would let him continue to keep her at a cold distance. "We're going to be spending months together," she said. "I want us to be friends. The last thing I want is to interfere with your operation. I know you have a job to do—don't resent me for doing mine."

Did she imagine the softening of his expression, a relaxing of the stiff line of his shoulders? "All right," he said gruffly.

She took a seat on a chaise and motioned for him to sit across from her on a similar lounge chair. "Let's have a drink and talk for a minute. Tell me what work you've done so far on the wreck of the *Eve*." She signaled to a waiting steward, who nodded and disappeared belowdecks.

"We only arrived at the island yesterday, and we're still waiting on a key piece of equipment." He sat on the side of the chaise, carefully, as if he feared it might collapse beneath him. "Tomorrow we'll start mapping the wreck site with GPS. It's important to pinpoint the location of the items and their relationship to one another before we begin bringing anything to the surface."

As he spoke, she saw him relax, the tight lines around his mouth disappearing, his whole posture less rigid. He was in familiar territory now—the professor lecturing an ignorant student. She was content to play along if it got him to open up to her. "How soon before the actual salvage work begins?" she asked.

"From a few days to a week. It depends on how many items we have to map."

The steward reappeared with their drinks—a beer for the professor and sparkling water in a champagne glass for her. It was too early in the day for her to begin drinking, but she had a reputation as a diva to maintain. Was there any field where image was more important than television? She smiled at him over the rim of her glass. "You won't even know I'm here."

His face flushed. "Sorry I came on so strong earlier. I'd just found out the water dredge I ordered has been delayed. Every extra day costs my backer money, so I'm feeling under the gun."

"How many people do you have working for you?"

"I have three interns from the university, and I've hired two brothers, Sam and Roger Murphy, to run most of the heavy equipment." He sipped the beer, then continued. "They've worked other wrecks like this, so they know what they're doing."

"And you think the *Eve* could be even more valuable?" She leaned forward, eager to hear more about the riches he expected to find. This was what her viewers wanted, and the kind of footage she was after.

His frown returned and she could almost feel the chill radiating from him. "I'm more interested in the historical value of the artifacts," he said. "The *Eve* is an important piece of maritime history. The items we recover can give us a clearer picture of life aboard a privateer vessel in the seventeenth and eighteenth centuries."

"You mean, a pirate ship. And don't tell me the thought of all that gold and silver and jewels doesn't make your heart jump a little. I know the university doesn't pay you enough to be totally unconcerned about wealth."

He looked away. "I never said I wasn't interested in money, only that it's not my primary interest." He drained the beer and set the mug on the deck beside the chair. "I'd better be going."

"Just when our conversation was getting so interesting?"

But he didn't answer, and she made no attempt to delay him further. She sat back in the chaise and sipped her drink, and pondered why her question about money had upset him so. Was it because as an academic he thought he ought to be above common greed? Did he make a habit of denying his vices—jealousy, greed…lust?

She sighed. It was going to be a long summer if he insisted on being so standoffish. As long as they were on this island together, no reason they shouldn't enjoy themselves. Of course, there were other men here who'd be willing to amuse her, she was sure, but she wanted Adam.

ADAM LEFT SANDRA feeling more annoyed than he'd been when he arrived. Why did that damn woman always rub him the wrong way? She hadn't been in the harbor an hour, and already it was happening—he ought to be focused on the salvage operation, and all he could think of was her.

He never should have let himself get involved with her last fall, but she'd caught him at a weak moment. He'd told himself this summer would be different. He'd be too focused on his work here on the island to let her tempt him. But five minutes in her company and she'd proved him wrong.

He hated complications in his life and in his work, and she was a big one, a diva who was clearly accustomed to men hopping when she said "jump." He didn't have the time or energy to waste on her, no matter how much his libido begged to differ.

Instead of returning to his own yacht, he steered his Zodiac to the *Caspian*. The 120-foot research vessel would serve as the main workboat for the expedition, as well as home to the interns and the Murphy brothers.

"Adam, I'm glad you're back." One of the interns, a twentysomething named Brent, who wore his black hair in a long ponytail, greeted him as soon as he stepped on deck. "I've been waiting for you."

"What do you need?" Adam forced himself to assume a more pleasant expression. He liked Brent and the other interns, Tessa and Charlie. They shared his passion for history and were willing to work all summer for low wages and the chance to make a little history of their own.

"I've got some bad news. The magnetometer is broken."

"What? It can't be." The magnetometer measured changes in the earth's magnetic field that indicated the presence of iron and other minerals that could point to artifacts beneath the layers of silt and sand on the ocean floor.

Brent looked grim. "Afraid so. When we unpacked it this morning, we discovered the glass was shattered. We'll have to send it back to Jamaica to be repaired. The captain of the *Caspian* already radioed for someone to come pick it up."

"We can't wait for it to be repaired. Send a message for the courier to bring a new one with him."

"Sure. That's a great idea." Brent hesitated. "How should I tell them we'll pay for it?"

"Charge it to Merrick." Damian Merrick, a science nut who also happened to be the heir to the Merrick semiconductor fortune, had agreed to finance the salvage of the *Eve*. In exchange, Adam had reluctantly agreed to send regular reports of the expedition's progress. He'd drawn the line at having Merrick as part of the operation. It was bad enough having Sandra hanging around. He didn't need two amateurs to babysit.

Adam and Brent made their way to the stern, where Tessa and the Murphy brothers were sorting diving equipment and other gear. Roger Murphy looked up at their approach. He was a short, stocky figure with faded red hair that looked as if it had been styled with a machete. "Hi, Professor," he said. "Checked the weather report?"

"No. Why?" Adam braced himself for more bad news.

"Looks good for the next few days, but there's a low-pressure system building off the coast of Africa that could bring trouble later in the week."

"Or it could be nothing," Adam said.

"I make it a point to keep an eye on the weather," Roger said. "I got caught in a hurricane off the coast of Haiti five years back and it's not an experience I care to repeat. I was nearly killed and the expedition lost almost everything."

"We'll be fine," Adam said. "When I was here last summer, it scarcely rained."

"Yeah, well, that was last summer."

Adam made no answer. It wasn't as if he wasn't concerned; his research had revealed that major hurricanes had hit the island in 1850, 1910 and 1941. Even a relatively minor storm would delay their operation by days, possibly weeks. But there was nothing he could do to control the weather, so he saw no profit in fretting over it.

"Any word on the water dredge?" he asked, changing the subject to a more pressing concern. "Is it here yet?"

"It arrived in Kingston today," Roger said. "It should be here day after tomorrow."

"We'll have to start the survey without it," Adam said. He addressed the interns. "Are you all ready to dive tomorrow?"

"I can't wait." Tessa, the only woman on the expedition, grinned up at him. "Just the thought of seeing the wreck up close makes me so excited."

Charlie muttered something under his breath. Adam thought it was something along the lines of *I'd like to get you excited.*

"What did you say, Charlie?" Tessa glared at him.

Charlie coughed and reached for a weight belt from the pile on the deck. "Just that I'm excited, too. About the wreck."

Adam rubbed his hand across his face in an attempt to wipe away a smile. He supposed he'd better have a talk with Charlie about sexual harassment, though the combination of raging hormones, scanty bathing suits and a summer in paradise almost guaranteed that various members of the crew would be hooking up. He only hoped the scarcity of women didn't lead to fighting among the men.

Tessa and Sandra were the only available women so far, unless Sandra had someone on board he didn't know about.

"How's our resident celebrity?" Sam Murphy spoke around the stub of an unlit cigar that was a fixture at the corner of his mouth.

"Celebrity?" Tessa raised a questioning look to Adam.

"That television babe, Sandra Newman," Sam said. "That's her yacht that just arrived. She's here to make movie stars of all of us." Sam laughed at his own joke, a harsh barking sound.

Tessa's eyes widened. "For real? Sandra Newman? Here?"

Adam nodded. "She's making a documentary about Passionata and her treasure. But she's promised not to interfere with our work."

"We'll get to meet her, won't we?" Tessa asked. "I saw her special on *Art Collections of the Rich and Famous.* She was awesome."

"What's she like?" Charlie grinned at Adam. "Is she as hot in person as she is on TV?"

Adam had the urge to wipe the leer off the kid's face. "Stay out of her way," he said. "She's got a job to do, and so do you."

Charlie executed a crisp salute. "Aye, aye, Captain. Didn't mean to poach on your territory."

"She's not my territory!" Heat flushed his face. Sandra had made it clear last fall that she viewed him as nothing more than a pleasant diversion, a sentiment he'd shared. He didn't have time for that sort of distraction while he was working, though he was having more difficulty putting her out of his mind than he'd anticipated. He didn't need Charlie—or anyone else—reminding him of what he was missing.

"She's not part of our crew," he continued. "The less we have to do with her the better."

Roger let out a low whistle. "I think we get the picture. So what did this Sandra woman do to get you so hot and bothered?"

"She didn't do anything."

Anything except throw him completely off balance from their second meeting. Their first meeting didn't really count; he'd been high on pain pills, still reeling from a nasty encounter with a shark while he'd been raising a demiculverin from the *Eve*. He rubbed his thigh where the scar still glowed an ugly white against his tan. When Sandra Newman had sailed into the harbor last summer aboard her fancy yacht, he hadn't known or cared who she was. He'd seen her as just one more interruption to his work.

But the next day, she'd shown up at his yacht when he was there alone, and the full force of her presence had hit him. From her gleaming fall of brunette hair to her red-painted toenails, Sandra Newman was a woman who screamed sex. Frankly, after a summer of celibacy watching his friend Nicole and the island's other occupant, an Englishman named Ian Marshall, make eyes at each other, Adam had probably been more vulnerable than usual to Sandra's come-ons.

"If you're not interested, maybe I'll row over and say hello." Sam winked at his brother, who chewed on his cigar and smirked. "In my free time, of course," he added.

"You're not going to have any free time," Adam said. "We start work first thing tomorrow." He turned and headed for the bridge to let the captain know he wanted to be at the wreck site at first light. But the men's laughter and comments about Sandra followed him.

The comments rankled because he knew more than mere lust lay at the root of his attraction to the beautiful reporter. When she'd wrapped her arms around him and pressed her lips to his, he'd felt a shock of recognition. As if he'd kissed this woman before. Many times. And liked every one of them very much.

Which was ridiculous. He'd never laid eyes on Sandra before they'd met on the island last summer, and she definitely wasn't the type of woman he ever associated with. He liked simple, uncomplicated women. Women with whom he enjoyed quiet, low-key affairs until it was time to move on. Women who didn't interfere with his work, who understood his devotion to both teaching and his treasure-hunting hobby.

Sandra was none of those things. One look at her perfect manicure, designer clothes and movie-star smile and any man with half a brain knew immediately that she was complex, complicated, demanding and self-centered. In Sandra's world, everything revolved around her. And the last thing Adam would ever be was a planet in someone else's orbit.

2

FAINT STREAKS OF PINK and gold painted the underside of low clouds the next morning when the dive boat anchored a short distance from the wreck site. Adam and his helpers carefully unpacked the equipment they'd need to begin mapping the shipwreck—grids, GPS unit, cameras and measuring sticks. The plan this morning was to begin documenting the debris field, measuring and photographing the area and plotting every possible artifact.

Adam, Tessa and Sam made the first dive, Adam leading the way toward the underwater canyon where the *Eve* had lain for over three hundred years. His heart raced and his breathing was loud and rapid in his ears as he swam toward the site he'd last seen ten months ago. Last night he'd dreamed he'd arrived at the canyon and the *Eve* was gone.

He kicked harder, rushing forward, Tessa and Sam on his heels. The three of them shot out over the canyon then floated, hovering over the remains of what Adam hoped to prove had been the *Eve*.

To the untrained eye, there was nothing remarkable below them—a pile of rocks, oddly shaped chunks of coral and protruding bits of rusted metal. But to the treasure hunter, these were the signs of a shipwreck. The wooden hull of the vessel had long since rotted away or been eaten by shipworms, but the rocks were the cobblestones once used as ballast in the ship's hold, the metal was the remains of anchor chains and keel bolts and the coral hid no telling what manner of treasure.

Tessa looked at him, eyes wide with excitement. Adam grinned and nodded that he understood. The thrill of touching a part of history never faded for him, even after all this time. Sam headed down toward the wreck and the others followed and set to work. They sank grids into the ocean floor, carefully brushed sand from artifacts and took dozens of photographs.

Adam was soon so absorbed in his work that when Sam tapped his shoulder, he jumped. He glared at the older man, who merely pointed across the canyon. Three dark figures hovered just above them.

He blinked, wondering if his eyes were playing tricks on him in the murky water. But the figures swam closer and now he could clearly make out Sandra with two men. One held a massive spotlight, the other a camera.

He handed Sam his own camera and went to intercept Sandra and her crew. Grabbing her shoulder, he motioned for her to surface with him so they could talk. She frowned and shook her head, but he nodded and once more pointed up.

As soon as they broke the surface of the water, Adam spat out his regulator and pushed down his mask. "What are you doing?" he demanded.

"I'm filming. That's why I'm here, remember?"

"I know that, but there's nothing to film yet. We're doing our preliminary measurements and photography." He had counted on having a few more days before he had to deal with her constant, distracting presence.

"My intent is to chronicle the salvage process," she said. "This is part of it, isn't it?"

He forced his eyes away from the top of her wet suit,

where the zipper strained across her breasts. The suit fit her like a second skin, emphasizing every curve. If he had to look at her like this every day for the rest of the summer, he might very well go mad. "Since when do you dive?" he asked.

"Since now. I took lessons in preparation for this trip." She leaned toward him, one hand on his shoulder. "I take my job very seriously, Adam. And I'm sure my viewers are interested in seeing every aspect of your work."

"There's nothing to film right now," he said again, the awareness of her touching him making him more loquacious than usual. If he could find the right words, maybe she'd leave him in peace. "This is the most boring part of the whole process. Though most of it's boring, really. Measuring. Sifting dirt—things like that." He gained confidence with every word. "In fact, what you should probably do is wait until the treasure is all up top. It will look much better up there, especially after it's cleaned up."

To his astonishment, she smiled—a dazzling smile that made him feel light-headed. "I know what you're doing," she said. "And it won't work. You won't get rid of me that easily. I'm staying for the *entire* salvage operation."

He was defeated. He knew it, though he'd never admit it. "When the salvage operation truly begins, I promise you'll get footage for your documentary. Until then, you're wasting film. Even *I* think this part is dull, but it's necessary."

She studied his face, her blue eyes searching, her lips slightly puckered, as though she were about to kiss him. The memory of other volcanic kisses they'd shared had him breathing hard—and his wet suit was getting uncomfortably tight below the waist.

She must have decided he was telling the truth. She took her hand from his shoulder and retreated a little.

"When does the exciting part of the work begin—when will I be able to show actual treasure to my viewers?" she asked.

"Several days at least. Maybe as long as a week."

"What am I supposed to do in the meantime?" Her tone was cool, all business.

"I don't know. Explore the island. Work on your tan. This is a tropical paradise. Take advantage of it."

"I didn't come here for a vacation," she said. "I came to work."

"So did I." He made a show of checking his watch. "And I'd better get back to it."

He started to fit his mask over his eyes again, but she put out her hand to stop him. "I'll leave you and your crew alone for now on one condition," she said.

"What's that?"

"You have dinner with me tonight and fill me in on your progress so far. And provide a similar report every day until the actual salvage work begins."

He had a sense of how the fly felt when invited for tea by the spider. "I don't have time for that," he protested.

"We have to work together, Adam." She rested her palm flat against his chest and leaned closer still, her mouth next to his ear. "So make time," she whispered.

Stunned, he watched as she pushed off and swam away, toward the Zodiac anchored nearby. In a moment the cameraman and his assistant surfaced also and the trio left. Sandra sat in the stern and waved as they motored away. "See you tonight," she called.

He shook his head, trying to clear it. If he believed in nonsense like witches, he'd say Sandra was one. She'd clearly cast a spell on him. He credited himself with being smart enough to avoid obvious hazards, including the wrong women. He couldn't think of a woman more wrong for him than Sandra, but he wasn't having any success in avoiding her.

"What was that about tonight?"

He looked behind him and was startled to see Sam treading water. "How long have you been listening?" Adam asked.

Sam smirked. "Long enough. Looks like our sexy reporter has the hots for you, you lucky dog."

Adam refused to take the bait. "What are you doing up here?" he snapped.

"Time to switch out crews."

Tessa joined them and they returned to the boat. Charlie, Brent and Roger went down to resume the work.

Adam was in the bow, changing his air tanks when Sam joined him. Adam glared at the older man. *One word about Sandra and I'll punch that smirk right off his face.* "What do you want?" he asked.

"Just one question." Sam crouched in the bow beside Adam. "Do we know for sure this is the *Eve?*"

Adam knew what Sam was getting at: any number of ships reportedly sank off the coast of Passionata's Island, the victims of either storms or attacks by the female pirate's gang. Adam was relying on a combination of research, hunches and instinct that told him this was Passionata's flagship. But instinct and hunches didn't carry much weight in the scientific community, and the research materials available were few. In his search for funding, he'd been careful to emphasize the historic nature of the material they were likely to find, while never stating that he was absolutely sure the wreck was that of the *Eve.*

"We don't know for sure what ship it is," he admitted. "That's one of the things I intend to find out."

"You think Ms. Newman will pitch a fit if she's gone to

all the trouble of bringing a film crew down here and it *isn't* the *Eve?*" Sam asked.

"I don't give a damn what Sandra Newman thinks," he said. "And don't you go stirring up trouble by saying anything about it. As far as she's concerned, we're salvaging the *Eve.*"

"Aye, aye, Captain." Sam saluted, then rose and sauntered away, whistling under his breath.

Adam turned back to the task of fitting his regulator to the new tanks. Yes, Sandra would no doubt create quite a scene if she thought he'd deceived her about the nature of the wreck. But as far as he was concerned, he had found the *Eve.* He'd felt it with a certainty that had been unshakeable ever since he'd first laid eyes on the debris scattered across the ocean floor, as if something in him had recognized the vessel. Call it instinct or memory or a sixth sense; it wasn't scientific or logical and he'd have never breathed a word to a soul that he harbored such thoughts. But he couldn't shake free of the belief. Like his fascination with Sandra, it hung around his neck like an albatross, a seaman's curse he'd have to learn to live with until he was proven right or defeated in his quest.

SANDRA FASTENED the necklace and stepped back from the mirror to check her outfit. The red silk gown draped softly over her breasts, nipped in at the waist, then fell in smooth gathers to the floor. A tiny golden globe glinted from its gold chain at her throat, and simple diamond studs glittered at her ears. The look was simple, elegant and sexy. She dared Adam to ignore her tonight.

She'd tried relating to him as a businesswoman and professional, but that clearly wasn't working. The air around them crackled with barely suppressed desire whenever the two of them were together. They might as well clear the air and give in to temptation. Some no-strings-attached hot sex would be just the thing to allow them to concentrate on their work—while passing their off hours in a most enjoyable manner.

It was just as Passionata had written in her autobiography, *Confessions of a Pirate Queen:* if a woman wanted to control a man, she should use all the gifts in her power, including her sexuality. The pirate queen had certainly done well following this philosophy, if even half of what she'd written was to be believed. And since Sandra and Adam were visiting Passionata's Island, well, when in Rome…

A knock distracted her. She hurried from the mirror and draped herself across a chair facing the door. "Come in," she called.

Adam had to duck to pass through the low cabin door. As he did so, he looked around warily, like a wild beast suspicious of a trap. "Hello, Sandra," he said, his gaze shifting to her then quickly away.

"Hello, Adam." She rose and took his hand. "Come inside and make yourself comfortable." She led him to a chair next to hers.

"I brought wine," he said, and thrust a dusty bottle toward her. "This *prosecco* was the closest I had to champagne."

That he'd remembered her preference surprised her; maybe the professor wasn't as absentminded as she'd thought. "Thank you. I love *prosecco.*" She carried the wine to a sideboard, opened it and poured two glasses.

"How did the rest of your survey work go today?" she asked.

"Slow." He sat back in the chair and sipped the wine. "It's not my favorite part of the job," he admitted. "I'm anxious to get to the real work of discovering and cataloging artifacts."

"I looked at the footage we shot this morning," she said. "You were right, it isn't very exciting. But I'll probably use a few seconds of it, to give viewers an idea of the scope of the job."

"I don't know much about television, but I don't see how there'll be enough of interest here to fill a whole hour or however long this show will be," he said.

"Given time for commercial breaks, about forty minutes." She settled in the chair beside his and tucked one leg under. "I think we'll have trouble covering everything in that time frame. I'd like to devote a portion of the show to Passionata and her story. If readers know about her, then her ship and its contents will seem that much more interesting to them."

"Why are *you* so interested in this wreck?" he asked. "Seems to me there are a lot of other things you could film a documentary about."

"I've made a name for myself filming stories about exotic riches—rare jewels and art, the lifestyles of the rich and decadent. What's more decadent than a sexy female pirate's treasures?"

"So it's the treasure that drew you."

She sipped her wine, trying to decide how honest she could afford to be with him. "The treasure, the larger-than-life characters, the drama of the salvage operation—all of that drew me. I needed something to dazzle the viewers, and the network."

"You mean, you alone aren't enough to dazzle them?"

The flattery startled her, until she saw the corner of his mouth twitch. She sighed. "Laugh if you want, but the ratings on my last special weren't as spectacular as the network wanted. And this project gives me the chance to do more. I'm not only reporting, I'm doing all the writing, directing and editing." The station had agreed to this plan because it saved them money, but she wanted to prove they'd underestimated her talent. She was more than just a pretty face and figure to pose in front of the camera, someone they could cast aside in favor of a younger and even more beautiful candidate. She hadn't clawed her way up from the weather girl on the third-ranked station in Oilton, Oklahoma, to let that happen. There was more than money or fame at stake here; her pride was on the line.

She fingered the charm she wore on a gold chain around her neck—a tiny golden globe. A reminder from her grandmother that the world could be hers, but she had to seize it. "No one hands you anything in this life," her grandmother had cautioned her as a child. "If you want something, you have to take it." Even as a young girl, Sandra had wanted more than the dull, small-town life she'd been born into. She'd worked hard to earn the wealth, glamour and excitement she'd longed for, but even that was never quite enough.

Another knock signaled the arrival of their dinner. "I thought we'd eat in here," she said as the steward wheeled in a white-draped table and an array of covered dishes. "It's much more private and intimate."

A muscle twitched in the corner of his mouth at the word *intimate,* and he shifted in his chair but remained silent.

When they were alone again, Sandra uncovered the food and invited him to sit. "I thought it would be fun to recreate the meal Passionata served the Duke of Brunswick-Luneburg," she said. "Oysters, roast beef, lobster pies, fried beets and potatoes." In *Confessions,* Passionata had claimed this was a meal designed to arouse and to provide strength for the night ahead.

"I doubt much of Passionata's—or as she was born, Jane Hallowell's—so-called autobiography was actually written by her," Adam said as he sat across from Sandra at the table.

"You do?" She didn't try to hide her surprise. "I thought *Confessions of a Pirate Queen* is what led you to the island and the shipwreck."

He shook his head. "I've read the book, of course, and I'm sure there's some fact there. But most of it is so sensationalized—like the account of her dinner with the future King George." He shook hot sauce onto an oyster and tossed it into his mouth.

"Then who do you think is the author?" she asked. She served herself some of the potatoes and some of the roast beef, avoiding the raw oysters—though she could admit a certain fascination in watching Adam swallow them with such relish.

He helped himself to another oyster before answering. "I think the book was probably written in the late eighteenth century by some unknown writer out to make a quick buck—much like the American dime novels. He—or she—had heard some stories about the notorious lady pirate and made the rest up. The addition of all the sex practically guaranteed a bestseller."

"So even in the 1700s, sex sold." She sliced into her roast and shook her head. "I don't agree that the book isn't Passionata's. I think the account rings true. At least, I believe it was written by a woman who knew what she was talking about."

"So you believe all that about women's power over men?" He looked amused, or perhaps that was only the effect of his second glass of wine.

"Don't you?" She laid aside her knife and fork and looked him in the eye.

"I believe women like to think they have that kind of power over men, but most of us aren't as susceptible as that."

"I don't know about that," she said. She could practically feel the heat arcing between them.

He took another long drink of wine and pretended interest in his food, though she was sure every part of him was as aware of her as she was of him. "Not that I didn't enjoy our time together before," he said. "But when I'm working, I work. I don't have time for anything that doesn't involve the salvage of the *Eve*."

"There's always time for sex," she said. "It's like eating or breathing."

"Ask anyone who knows me and they'll tell you I scarcely take time for *those* things when I'm involved in a project." He pushed his empty plate away and crumpled his napkin beside it. "Thanks for dinner. Now I'd better get back to work."

"But you haven't had dessert," she said. She stood and walked slowly back to the chairs where they'd started the evening, aware of his eyes on her, caressing her back and gliding over her hips. Smiling, she sat and removed the cover from a small dish on the table between the two chairs. "Strawberries," she said. "My favorite." She selected a large, ripe fruit and bit into it, her tongue darting out to lick the juices that dripped from her chin. "You must stay and have some," she said, her voice pitched just above a whisper, so that he had to lean forward to hear her.

"I'd really better go," he said, but made no move to leave.

"Please don't," she said. "Stay a little longer." The words were a line she'd rehearsed in her head, but even she heard the earnestness in her voice when she spoke them. The truth was, she did want Adam to stay. As rough and even rude as he sometimes was, he fascinated her.

And tempted her. While her intent had been to arouse him, she was more than a little turned on herself. Somewhere between the first glass of wine and the disappearance of the last oyster, he'd become not merely a man she wanted to control, but a man she *wanted.*

EVERY INSTINCT told Adam to bolt for the door, but he remained fixed in place, mesmerized by the sight of Sandra's moist, full lips caressing the ripe fruit. Her every action was incredibly over the top, yet intoxicatingly alluring.

With one finger she caught a drop of juice that dripped from the berry, and sucked it from her finger. He drew in a sharp breath and felt his groin tighten. Their eyes locked and the raw wanting he saw there rocked him.

He shoved himself out of the chair and lurched toward the door. "Good night," he muttered, avoiding looking at her as he passed.

"No, wait." She caught him by the wrist, her fingers tightening around him. "I…" She released him and touched her temple. "I don't feel so well."

At first he suspected another ploy to delay him, but one look at her had him doubting that anyone could be such an accomplished actress. Her skin had turned dead white, and her eyes held a distant expression. "What is it?" he asked, alarmed. "What's wrong?"

"I don't know. I…" Before she could complete the sentence, she slumped forward in the chair.

He lunged to grab her before she slid to the floor. He tried to prop her up in the chair once more, but she'd gone completely limp, unable to support herself. He ended up cradling her in his arms, her head lolling against his shoulder. He looked around for some bell or button to use to summon help, but saw nothing. He could step into the corridor and shout, but that would mean leaving her and he was afraid to do so for even that little bit.

At least she was still breathing, her chest rising and falling steadily. He was relieved to see that some of the color had returned to her skin, her cheeks flushed a soft pink. At this close proximity, the soft floral scent of her hair engulfed him. Her lips were slightly parted, her lashes a heavy fringe just brushing her cheeks. Inert like this, her face without its usual animation, she looked surprisingly small and delicate.

Vulnerable.

Desirable.

He pushed the thought away. Maybe she was suffering from too much to drink, though like him, she'd only had two glasses of wine. Unless she'd had some before he'd arrived.

In any case, he had to make her more comfortable. Settling her more firmly in his arms, he searched the cabin for someplace to lay her. He spotted a door to his right and pushed it open.

The small stateroom was awash in red—red draperies, red wallpaper, red floral comforter on the bed. Adam laid Sandra on the bed and wondered if he should loosen her clothes. The thought of undressing her made him feel shaky. Better not go there. Her dress fit her well, but it wasn't overly tight.

Very carefully, he sat on the edge of the bed and took her wrist in his hand, feeling for her pulse. It was rapid but strong. Should he call someone? But who? There was no doctor on the island. He wished his friend Nicole was here. Not only was she another woman, she was a nurse. She'd know how to handle the situation.

He touched Sandra's cheek, so soft and smooth. She really was the most beautiful woman... Resolutely, he pulled his thoughts back to more practical matters and patted her jaw. "Sandra," he said. Then louder, "Sandra, can you hear me? Wake up."

Her eyes fluttered and she stared at him, her pupils dilated, her breathing more rapid than ever. "Thank God you're here," she whispered.

"I didn't do anything but keep you from hitting your head when you fell. What happened?"

"Happened?" She blinked. "Nothing's happened. Yet." She smiled and slid her hand up his arm. "I'm so glad to see you," she said. "I've missed you so much."

"Missed me? I've been right he—"

His words were smothered by her lips on his. With surprising strength, she pulled him to her, wrapping her arms around him, opening her mouth to him. She was so warm and soft and willing… For a moment he forgot where he was. *Who* he was. He wasn't an almost-forty-year-old academic who preferred study to socializing, and research to relationships; he was a hedonist who knew what it was to make love to a woman until they were both fully sated and exhausted. A man whom a woman like Sandra would beg to be with.

She squirmed beneath him, and he put out a hand to steady her, encountering the soft, supple curve of her breast. He shaped his hand to her and squeezed gently, her soft cry of delight recalling him to his senses.

He pushed out of her embrace, horrified at his actions. What was he doing fondling a woman who was clearly out of her head? As much as he'd previously enjoyed sex with Sandra, he wasn't going to take advantage of her when she wasn't in her right mind.

"Frederick, don't go!" She protested. "Don't leave me when I want you so badly." She arched her body in flagrant invitation.

Adam was having trouble breathing. *Who the hell is*

Frederick? he wanted to ask. Was she so drunk she couldn't remember his name?

But she didn't act drunk exactly. She acted more— crazy. She stared at him with unabashed passion. He couldn't remember when a woman had ever looked at him that way, and once again he was tempted to strip off his clothes and join her on that red comforter.

"Frederick, please," she moaned, and the words brought him back to his senses. Even he wasn't desperate enough to sleep with a woman who couldn't get his name right. Though right now Adam could admit he was jealous of Frederick, whoever he was.

"I'll send someone to check on you," he said as he backed out the door. Tomorrow she might have a hell of a hangover, but he hoped for both their sakes, she wouldn't remember any of this had happened.

3

FOG SURROUNDED Sandra, obscuring her vision, clouding her thoughts. She had a vague memory of sitting in a chair, drinking wine with...someone. She couldn't remember. Then she was sinking into oblivion, waking yet not waking to the sensation of strong arms wrapped around her, carrying her to a bed.

Deft hands undressed her. Masculine hands, with strong fingers that caressed her naked breasts and stroked her bare thighs with a shocking possessiveness. She opened her mouth to protest, but could only sigh as his touch aroused a pleasure unlike any she had ever known. She reached for him, calling his name. "Frederick."

How did she know his name? She couldn't see his face, couldn't bring it to mind. Yet his touch was familiar to her. More than familiar, it was something she craved, *needed,* in a way she had never needed anything before.

He stretched beside her on the bed, naked also. She had a sense of muscular limbs, of the weight of him pressing her into the comforter, his hands parting her thighs, stroking her, fingers plunging inside her. She arched to him, shamelessly begging for more.

He reached one hand to fondle her breasts, plucking at one nipple, then the next. Desire lanced through her, sharp and urgent. She raised her head, desperate to see his face, but saw only a shock of blond hair.

He was skilled and masterful, anticipating the touch that would arouse her most, his fingers playing across her clit, bringing her to the edge of release but no further. She writhed beneath him, wild with wanting, beyond caring who he was or how he knew her, wanting only the ecstasy he promised yet withheld.

Then he was pushing her back again, spreading her legs farther, plunging into her with a force that stole her breath. He filled her completely, perfectly, the rhythm of advance and retreat sending her spiraling upward again. She clutched handfuls of the comforter beneath her, the silky fabric bunching in her hands as he rode her, his face still lost to her in the haze she couldn't shake.

She gave up fretting about it, surrendered everything to the tension growing within her. He moved faster, thrusting harder, and brought his hand down to fondle her clit once more.

At his touch, she shattered, crying out as heat and light flooded her, leaving her trembling, fully sated. She felt the clench and release of his muscles as he met his own climax, and held him tightly as he shuddered in her arms.

A profound weariness filled her, and she closed her eyes and slept, still clinging to her mystery lover, praying he would never leave.

SANDRA WOKE TO SUNLIGHT spilling from the porthole in her cabin, a dull ache in the back of her head, her thoughts a kaleidoscope of broken images. She frowned, trying to concentrate. She'd had dinner last night with Adam. They had drunk the wine he'd brought and then…

Heat flooded her face as memories of wild sex with a faceless stranger filled her. Had that been Adam?

She sat up, alarmed, and discovered she was still dressed in the red gown she'd chosen last night and that she lay on top of the comforter, which had half slid to the floor. There was no sign of the professor—no note, no indentation on the pillows other than her own.

Had it all been a dream, then? She pushed her hair back from her face and tried to concentrate. The fog, the faceless man, her own passiveness—they all pointed to a dream. Though one of the most vivid and erotic dreams she had ever experienced. She was sure she'd climaxed. Was that even possible? Men had wet dreams, but could women?

She shook her head and carefully crawled out of bed. The headache was already abating, and she felt none of the queasiness that signaled a hangover. But she had no memory of anything after she'd begun to eat the strawberries she'd chosen for dessert.

Had Adam put something in her wine to knock her out? One of the date-rape drugs she'd reported on that rendered their victims helpless? But why would he do that? It wasn't as if she hadn't already been a perfectly willing partner....

She stumbled into the bathroom and stripped off her clothes, checking carefully for any sign that she'd been molested. But her underwear was still in place; she bore no bruises. And beyond all that was her conviction that Adam wouldn't do something like that. He had to know that if he wanted her, all he had to do was ask. He had no need to drug her.

She turned on the shower and stepped inside, raising her face to the hot spray. Maybe she'd had a bad reaction to something they'd eaten. She'd heard certain toxins could cause hallucinations. Could they also cause erotic dreams? She smiled. If so, maybe she should figure out what food had been the culprit and eat it again. She didn't know if she'd ever had a real sexual encounter as intense as the one she'd dreamed.

She poured shampoo into her palm and lathered it into her hair. The dream had been odd in others ways, too. Disturbing even. Her dream self had been completely dominated by the mystery man, content to let him take charge, eager even to submit to him. The idea that such desires hid in her subconscious annoyed her. She wasn't a passive woman and had no wish to be. If anything, *she* preferred to take the lead in her relationships with men. In her experience it was the only way to keep them from underestimating her.

She rinsed her hair and body, then stepped out of the shower, her thoughts turning once more to Adam. She'd have to ask him for his version of last night's events and see what he had to say. She checked the clock and saw that it was after ten o'clock. Too late to question Adam now. He'd be at the wreck site, continuing his survey. A survey she hoped he'd finish soon. She was anxious to get to work.

What was she supposed to do with herself in the meantime? She looked around the stateroom, hoping for something that would strike her interest, but found nothing. Then her gaze rested on the view through the porthole—a vista of Passionata's Island. That was it then; she'd explore the former pirate's stronghold, maybe even take along a camera and get some footage of the tower. If she found anything particularly interesting, she could send Jonas to film more later.

Cheered by the idea, she dressed in an orange bikini, then added khaki shorts and a shirt over that. With tennis shoes and hat, she was ready to discover what it was that had attracted a woman like Passionata to this beautiful but desolate place.

ADAM RESISTED THE URGE to visit Sandra's ship and make sure she was all right after the strange events of the previous night. He couldn't think of any way to do so without calling attention to himself among the crew; they were already giving him a hard enough time about having dinner with the celebrated news personality.

He tried to ignore their jibes and off-color comments. He'd been around long enough to know he made an easy target. He was a workaholic, careless of his appearance— an unlikely choice for a glamorous woman like Sandra.

But there'd been no mistaking her physical interest in him. He couldn't deny the idea flattered him. Intrigued him. He wasn't a man who'd lacked for female companionship, but Sandra was definitely in another league from the quiet, bookish types he preferred.

In any case, he hoped she was all right. He had no intention of mentioning her odd behavior of the night before. Maybe she *had* been drunk.

As soon as he was out on the water, headed to the wreck site, he put all thoughts of Sandra aside. This was what he'd lived the past ten months for, this chance to touch a part of history, to uncover things no one else had seen in three hundred years, to make all the words written in the books lining his office at the university come to life.

As an only child whose parents worked long hours, Adam's chief amusements had been reading and exploring the stretch of woods behind the housing development where his family lived. He'd occupied himself for entire summers imagining elaborate scenarios where he discovered dinosaur bones or lost civilizations. To realize those boyhood dreams as an adult was the greatest thrill he could enjoy. That the pursuit of that goal had left him little time for long-term relationships with women hadn't mattered to him so far. Work had given him everything he needed in his life.

"Who makes the first dive today?" Roger asked as he anchored the dive boat.

"I'll work with Tessa," Charlie volunteered.

Tessa made a face. "I'd rather work with Adam."

"You and Charlie and Brent should work together," Adam said. "Continue marking the grid on the east side of the debris field."

"What are you going to be doing?" Roger asked.

"I'm going to get a better look at the far side of the canyon," he said. "We haven't done much exploring there yet. There may be artifacts spread out in that area, as well."

When he was satisfied the interns had everything they needed to do their job, Adam headed for the far side of the underwater canyon where the bulk of the wreck rested. The ocean floor sloped down, and as he swam deeper the water grew cooler and darker. He switched on the spotlight he carried and played it along the ocean floor, searching for anything out of place. An odd-shaped rock could be a sediment-covered bottle, a glint of metal might reveal a coin and a bump on the ocean floor might turn out to be a cannonball. He had discovered early on that he had a good eye for these oddities, and a sixth sense for what was treasure and what was trash.

As the spotlight cut through the dimness, revealing brightly colored fish and the undulations of the underwater terrain, Adam felt a deep peace settle over him. This was the part of his work he loved most, losing himself in new discoveries, seeing things as few others saw them.

Out of the corner of his eye he caught a glint of something and quickly focused the light in that direction. At first he saw nothing, but as he swam closer, he noticed an irregularity in the ocean floor. He reached down and carefully fanned away the top layer of sediment, revealing a jeweled dagger. It lay in the gravel as if only recently dropped there by some passing sailor, its blade darkened, the red stone in its hilt glowing dully.

His heart raced as he fumbled with his free hand for his camera. He snapped a few pictures, then took out his GPS to read the coordinates. These noted, he finally allowed himself to pick up the dagger, scarcely breathing as he cradled it in his hand.

It was heavy, yet perfectly balanced, the blade long and tapered. Cleaned and sharpened, it would be a deadly weapon, as well as a work of art. Through layers of grime, he thought he detected engraving, and filigreed metal surrounded the stone.

It was exactly the sort of thing Sandra would love to show her viewers.

That he would think of her in such a moment startled him so much he almost dropped the dagger. He gripped it more firmly, and tried to get a grip on his emotions, as well. This was a testament to the degree the sexy reporter had insinuated herself into his life in such a short time.

So far he'd been successful in keeping thoughts of last night away, but now the memories flooded back. The way she'd looked at him after he'd carried her to bed, as if her very *life* depended on him making love to her, had unnerved him. The Sandra he knew was not the type to humble herself to anyone, yet in those moments he had sensed she would have done anything he asked. And he couldn't deny that he'd wanted to ask. His desire for her had been overpowering, conquered only by his knowledge that he'd be taking advantage of a woman who clearly wasn't right in the head.

Walking away from her last night was one of the most difficult things he'd ever done, and chances were she wouldn't even remember his act of chivalry. Worse, he had no confidence he'd be as strong the next time she came on to him. His reluctance to get involved with Sandra while he had so much work to do was no match for the fierce physical pull he felt for her, whether she was out of her mind or not.

SANDRA BEACHED the Zodiac and made her way along the shore, searching for the path that led into the jungle. The wind had come up, and she had to hold on to her hat with one hand to keep it from being snatched away. Sand sifted into her shoes, so she took them off, sinking her toes into the hot, powdery beach. Maybe instead of exploring, she should take Adam's other suggestion, and work on her tan.

But the idea of sunning on the beach held little appeal with no beach chair or umbrella, no one to fetch her drinks and no one to lie with. She glanced toward Adam's yacht, anchored in the harbor. There was no sign of movement on the tarp-shaded deck. She thought of going aboard and waiting for him. What would he think if he returned from a day of diving and found her there? What if she were naked in his bed? Would he dare turn her away then?

She clenched her thighs against the rush of desire this fantasy produced. And she thought again of her dream last night. Had the skillful lover she'd imagined been Adam?

She shook her head. No matter what games her subconscious played, when she and Adam had made love before, it had been as equals. She would never play the shivering virgin for any man, and certainly not for a sloppy—though sexy—professor.

She spotted the path and stopped to put on her shoes. Despite her disdain for all the scary stories Adam and his friends had once told her about the dangerous wildlife on the island, she had no desire to step on one of the ever-present land crabs or, worse, a spider.

Once she started down the path, the dense undergrowth muffled the sound of the wind and blotted out all but the weakest rays of the sun, which filtered through the canopy overhead, bathing her in a watery green light. The air was heavy and humid, redolent with the scent of growth and decay. Though last summer the jungle had been hacked away to allow space for the passage of two people walking side by side, new growth crowded in on both sides, so that Sandra could barely squeeze through in places.

As she neared the center of the island, the noise of the birds increased, a cacophony of screams and whistles and honks louder than any freeway gridlock or rock concert riot. Along with the noise came the stench of the thousands of birds that nested and fed on the rocky heart of the island. Sandra covered her mouth and nose with one hand and held on to her hat with the other, the video camera swinging from the strap at her wrist, hitting her shoulder with every step.

Passionata's Tower rose from the center of the clearing, a squat, crenelated fortress three stories tall, built of the same gray volcanic rock as its surroundings, the surface pocked with white bird droppings. On an elevated platform beside it sat a large tank to collect rainwater, the only source of fresh water on the island. Last summer, some visitors had constructed a gravity-fed shower beneath the tank. It had provided a nice alternative to the cramped bathing quarters on board ship, and helped to conserve the fresh water they'd brought with them.

Sandra paused at the edge of the clearing and focused the camera, pleased with the shot of the tower rising up against a dramatic bank of threatening clouds. One of the afternoon squalls common during the summer months was blowing in. Exactly what was needed to add interest to her video.

Satisfied she'd captured some good exterior footage, she darted across the clearing to the shelter of the tower entrance. Birds whirled and screamed around her, and she resisted the urge to run away from them.

Once in the tower things were better, though the stench was worse than ever. She pulled her shirt up over her nose and mouth and turned to investigate the three-hundred-year-old structure.

Interest soon displaced distaste as she surveyed the space in which she was standing. A short passage from the doorway opened into a spacious round room or hall. Weather-worn rock provided both flooring and walls, but Sandra could imagine a time when the rock had been covered with tapestries or velvet drapes, the floor strewn with rugs woven in India and Turkey.

A stone stairway hugged the far wall. After filming the first floor, Sandra started up the narrow risers, following them around the outer wall to a second room that was almost as large as the first. Empty except for a few pieces of driftwood and a pile of shells some previous visitor had left behind, this would have been the public rooms that served as an office/living/dining area for the pirate queen. A single rectangular window six feet tall and three feet wide provided a spectacular view of the bay. From here Passionata could have seen the approach of any ship, whether friend or foe. She'd have welcomed the return of her own fleet, and prepared for battle with her enemies.

Sandra raised her camera to her eye and filmed the stark interior, imagining it furnished with a heavy carved table and chairs, and cushions on the window seat. She could almost smell beeswax candles burning.

With growing anticipation, she hurried up the final flight of stairs to the room at the top of the tower. This would have been Passionata's bedroom, she was sure. This room was smaller than the other two, but featured two windows, one looking out on the harbor, the other in the direction of the coral reef just offshore.

She stepped into the room as lightning flashed and rain began to fall. Large drops pelted the tower and splashed through the windows to pool on the concrete floor. Thunder shook the air and Sandra startled and backed up against the wall. Laughing at her own jumpiness, she raised the camera and began filming this room, as well, turning in a slow circle to take it all in.

Out of the corner of her eye, she caught a flash of red, and lowered the camera to look. But only gray stone met her gaze. Blinking, she shook her head, suddenly dizzy. The sweet scent of lavender filled her nostrils. Did lavender grow on the island? Had the rain brought the scent into the room?

She closed her eyes a moment and leaned against the wall, trying to regain her equilibrium. She put one hand down to steady herself, then recoiled at the sensation of some soft fabric, like a brocade.

She opened her eyes again and stared at a massive canopy bed that occupied the center of the room. It was draped in mosquito netting, the mattress covered with a red satin comforter much like the one she had on the ship. The concrete of the floor was obscured by a thick layer of red and gold rugs, and red draperies fluttered at the windows.

Her heart raced, and she struggled to breathe as she stared at the scene. None of this had been here seconds before. Was she hallucinating? She pinched her thigh, hard, but though she flinched at the pain, the room remained richly furnished. The scent of lavender was stronger now, almost overwhelming in its intensity. Her head began to throb, and she rubbed her eyes. What was happening to her?

She opened her eyes again, and choked off a scream. Gray stone walls and gray concrete floors surrounded her. The rain continued to pour in through the window, bringing the scent of mud and fish and tropical foliage. But no lavender.

She turned and raced down the stairs, moving as fast as she dared down the narrow risers, heart thudding painfully, fighting panic.

It was raining hard by the time she emerged from the tower. The birds were silent, roosting, the only noise the wind rattling the palm branches and raindrops splattering on the rocks. Within seconds, she was drenched, but she scarcely noticed. She had to get away from here, back to the safety of her ship.

She started toward the path, but a blinding flash of lightning and crack of thunder stopped her. One of the tall coconut palms split in two, crashing at her feet, green coconuts falling around her like bombs.

Her scream rose above the sound of the storm, and once she'd started, she couldn't make herself stop. Shrieks rose from her throat, an almost welcome release of the panic she'd been fighting. She was soaked through, shaking and absolutely terrified. The only consolation was there was no one here to see her falling apart.

"Sandra! What are you doing out here in the storm?"

The shouts startled her. She whirled and saw a man advancing toward her, a tall, broad-shouldered figure, his features blurred by the rain. Unsure whether this was another hallucination, she squinted, trying to bring him into sharper focus. He was closer now, and she made out dark-blond hair plastered to his head—hair like her dream man's. Her gaze moved across his shoulders, down his chest…he was naked, rain running in rivulets across well-defined muscle, glistening on the dusting of hair on his chest and between his thighs.

"Sandra, what are you doing here?" he demanded again. "Are you all right?"

He took her by the arm and shook her gently, and for the first time she realized this was no phantom of her imagination, but Adam, and he was very wet. And very naked.

4

ADAM SHOOK Sandra's shoulder again. She was starting to scare him, she looked so out of it. "What are you doing out here in the rain?" he asked.

She blinked at him, then seemed to pull herself together. "A better question is what are *you* doing out here, *naked?*"

He let go of her as if he'd been scorched and tried to look dignified—not an easy task considering he was indeed naked. "I was taking a shower," he said. "We had to knock off early because of the weather. When I heard you scream, I ran out without thinking."

"How gallant of you." She pushed a dripping strand of hair out of her eyes.

"This is ridiculous," he said. "Let's get out of the rain." Not waiting for her answer, he took her by the arm and led her to the shower underneath the tower's cistern, where he grabbed his swim trunks and now-sodden towel. Then he pulled her toward the tower.

She balked at the door. "I can't go in there," she said.

"You can't stand out here in the rain, either," he said, and tugged her inside.

While he pulled on the swim trunks, she stood just inside the door, hugging herself and looking around apprehensively. "What's wrong?" he asked. "I promise if any spiders or rats live here, they aren't interested in you."

"I'm not worried about spiders and rats." She looked up at the ceiling. "This place gives me the creeps."

He moved closer and stared at her intently. Her face was pale, her eyes slightly dilated, as if she was terrified— or on something. "What's wrong?" he asked. "You're acting strange."

This comment earned him an angry look. "I've been feeling strange since last night," she said. "Did you put something in my drink? A drug or something?"

He stared at her. "You think I *drugged* you? Glad to know you have such a high opinion of me. Just because I refused to sleep with you again doesn't make me some lowlife degenerate."

"What am I supposed to think when I was fine before you showed up for dinner and ever since I've been…" Her voice trailed off and she looked away.

"You've been what?"

"Not myself."

That was one way to put it. "You were acting oddly when I left you last night," he said. "I thought maybe you'd had too much to drink."

"I'd only had two glasses of wine. The wine *you* brought."

"I had that wine, too, and I'm fine."

"What exactly was I doing when you left last night?"

"You don't remember?"

She shook her head. "I don't really remember anything after eating the strawberries."

"You called me Frederick."

She frowned. "I don't know anyone named Frederick."

"Are you sure? No old boyfriend?"

"I'm sure. I don't even know anyone named Fred."

"That's definitely the name you used."

"That's all that happened? I called you Frederick?"

He tried to keep back the smile but couldn't. The memory of her writhing on that red satin comforter and begging for him was too pleasant. "You tried very hard to get me to come to bed with you."

She wet her lips, her eyes searching his. "Did I succeed?"

"The offer was tempting, but I decided not to take advantage of a woman who was obviously out of her head."

She turned and began pacing, agitation evident in every movement. "I had a very vivid dream last night. I was with a man whose face I couldn't see. And then this afternoon, here in the top room of the tower…"

"What happened?"

She stopped with her back to him, her head bent. "I had a hallucination. One moment the room was bare, the next it was furnished, with a bed and red draperies and carpets. It all seemed so real."

He frowned. "Do you think it was something you ate? Some hallucinogenic toxin in food?"

"You ate the same food—except the oysters. Have *you* been hallucinating?"

"No." He'd been fantasizing about her, but that wasn't the same. "Has anything like this happened to you before?" he asked.

"Never." She whirled to face him. "And if you tell a soul, I'll insist it's because you drugged me."

"I won't tell anyone." It stung that she'd think him that low. "You don't seem to have a very high opinion of me," he said. "First you think I'd drug you, now you think I'll go telling your private business to the world."

She bowed her head and took a deep breath. "I'm sorry. You don't deserve this. I really don't know what to think about any of this."

"Maybe you should go back to the States and have a doctor check you out."

"Why? Because you think I'm cracking up? Or because you'd love not having me and my film crew in your way?"

Again she made him sound like a jerk. Though maybe he had been a little bit of a hard-ass about her filming him. The truth was, he'd agreed to the documentary and accepted her station's money, so he had no right to complain. "When you know me better, you'll learn to ignore anything I say when I'm focused on a job," he said. "I really don't mind having you here. And my intern, Tessa, probably appreciates having another woman around."

"I haven't met Tessa yet. In fact, I haven't met any of your interns or crew."

"I guess we should have some kind of get-together where we all can meet." He scratched his head. "I'm not used to having to think about these things."

She tilted her head, studying him. "There has to be more in your life than work," she said, relaxing. "Tell me about what you do when you're not teaching or sailing."

"I read and do research. For the past two years I've been searching for the *Eve* and planning this trip."

"But what do you do for *fun?*"

He'd known she wouldn't understand; few people did. "I enjoy my research," he said, trying not to sound defensive.

"But don't you have a social life? Friends. *Women?*"

"Of course I have all those things." He went out with other professors at the university, and people like his long-time friend, Nicole, though she was in England with her new boyfriend, Ian, now.

"So you have a girlfriend waiting back home?"

"No. I'm not seeing anyone in particular right now." His last serious relationship had been with one of the secretaries in the dean's office, a single mother who took night classes with the intent of earning a degree in accounting. It had been a low-key affair. He never spent the night at her house because of her children, but he'd sometimes show up early on Saturdays and fix things around the house or they'd all spend the day at a ballpark. He'd been comfortable with her until she'd started hinting at wanting to make their situation more permanent. He couldn't see himself in that role, and they'd broken things off. Since then he'd been too busy to date. "Most women don't like to compete with my work," he said.

She looked at him intently, as if she could see past his outer self to his very thoughts. He began to feel nervous and had to fight the urge to step away. "So you don't believe there's any woman who could distract you from your work," she said.

"I didn't say that." *She'd* been distracting him plenty lately.

She moved closer, her voice low. Seductive. "You said you were tempted to take me up on my invitation to come to bed with me last night."

"Yes. You're a very tempting woman."

She laid her hand on his chest, her palm flat over his heart. "Then why are you so set against us enjoying ourselves while we're on the island?" She laughed. "I'm not expecting you to marry me, for goodness' sake."

"I told you. I have a lot of work to do. I don't like to be distracted."

"I'd think being horny all the time would be far more distracting than knowing you had a good time waiting at the end of the day." She moved her index finger up and down, stroking him. "We had a good time together last fall, didn't we?"

He couldn't think straight when she was so near. Her

argument sounded so logical, his so lame. His first instinct was to tell her he hadn't come to the island to have fun, but that made him sound like the worst sort of dork—someone he'd never hang out with and certainly not someone he intended to *be*. Besides, if they both accepted that they'd be together only for the duration of this project, they could avoid messy complications.

She moved her hand up higher, caressing his neck. "You can't deny there's a certain *chemistry* between us. A connection. I can't explain it, but then, I don't see any need to. Why not just enjoy ourselves?"

Why not, indeed? Away from her, he'd probably be able to think of a dozen reasons, but here alone with her, the rain walling them off from the rest of the world, his body had overwhelmed all attempt at reason. He wanted Sandra more than he'd ever wanted any woman.

She stood on tiptoe and pulled his head down to hers. When their lips met, his arms automatically went around her. There was nothing frantic in this embrace and nothing tentative. It was the leisurely kiss of experienced lovers, though perhaps lovers long parted; he couldn't deny the urgency with which he delved his tongue between her lips, or the strength of his desire as evidenced by the erection that swelled the front of his swim trunks.

In his arms she was pliant and playful, everything about her fascinating. When he began to unbutton her shirt, she stepped away from him, teasing him with the slow unveiling of her body. First the shirt, one button at a time, until he was all but panting to see what lay underneath.

Then the shorts, sliding oh-so-slowly down her shapely legs. She kicked off her sandals, then slid her thumbs in either side of the bikini bottoms. "Should I take them off?" she asked.

"If you don't, I will."

She removed her thumbs and crossed her arms over her chest. "I don't know. I think you should go first."

"Fine by me." He untied the drawstring of the trunks and shoved them to his ankles, then stood before her, naked and aroused, and feeling only a little like a piece of merchandise on display, waiting to see if he met with her approval.

The way she looked at him was worth any momentary embarrassment, though. He'd never had a woman look at him with such an expression of awe and wonder—as if she'd never seen a naked man before. Which was absurd. And it wasn't as if he was hung like a horse or something. He was a perfectly average man. Then again, maybe she'd been dating a lot of losers lately.

"What do you want me to do now?" she asked.

At first he thought she was teasing again, then he saw her whole posture had changed. She was standing sideways to him, trying to cover herself with her arms, as if she was truly embarrassed.

This had to be playacting on her part, though. She definitely wasn't the type to be shy in the bedroom. But he'd play along. It might even be fun.

Sandra watched as Adam advanced toward her. "I'm naked, so I think you ought to be, too," he said, as he reached behind her and undid the clasp on her bathing suit top.

She shivered as cool air rushed over her, puckering her nipples. She'd been fine, relaxed even, but now she felt so odd. Not dizzy, exactly, but as if she was hovering over her body, watching from a long way off. She tried to cover herself with her arms, and Adam gently pushed them aside. Why was she behaving this way? She felt almost…embarrassed. But why? She *wanted* him to look at her. Wanted to enjoy the expression on his face as he admired her. Men liked to look at her—and she liked them to look.

Yet here she was, uncharacteristically reluctant. She couldn't seem to stop herself. Almost as if she *wasn't* herself.

Adam didn't seem to notice. He was focused on her breasts, shaping his palms to them, lifting them, his calluses dragging across the sensitive tips, sending spirals of sensation to pool between her thighs.

When his mouth closed over her right breast, she gripped his shoulder tightly, sure her legs would give way if she didn't hold on. He sucked hard, the pressure pulsing in her groin, a second heartbeat.

She wanted to touch him, to wrap her fingers around his cock and feel how much he wanted her, but her hands refused to obey the impulse. She could feel the length of him pressed against her side, a heated iron branding her flesh.

He transferred his attention to the other breast, and she closed her eyes, surrendering to the flood of heat and need that assailed her.

The floating feeling became stronger. She felt helpless to do anything but accept whatever Adam did to her. It was a role so unlike her, yet his every touch sent such intense pleasure through her, she couldn't complain.

His mouth lingering at her breasts, he pushed her bikini bottoms to her ankles and steadied her as she stepped out of them and kicked them away. He parted her legs with a nudge of his knee and drew her close to ride his thigh. "There's nowhere to lie down," he said, his mouth against her neck. "We'll have to stand."

"It's all right," she said. She tightened her legs around him, desperate to ease the tension that radiated through her. "Just tell me what you want me to do."

Even as she said the words, something inside of her protested. *She* was the one who should be telling *him* what to do. Men *needed* direction from their partners. Otherwise, they were inclined to take things too quickly, cheating the woman out of her full measure of pleasure. Why take that chance?

But she was unable to make her lips form the words.

Adam needed no direction, however. He began to lay a path of kisses down her torso, across her stomach, until his mouth rested on her clit. He knelt before her, hands on her hips, and while she swayed above him, he began to caress her with his mouth.

Every sensation felt new, as if a man had never done this to her before. He stroked and suckled, teased and petted, until her legs trembled and her hands shook and she was sure she couldn't bear for him to continue another second, yet knew she would die if he did not.

He thrust his tongue into her, then drew the tight bud of her clit into his mouth, a final onslaught that made her come apart. She buried her fingers in his hair and screamed, a joyous, exultant cry.

While the sound still echoed around them he stood and put his hands on her shoulders. "Turn around," he said, his voice rough.

She did as he asked, and he pressed on her back, bending her over. Legs apart, she braced her hands against the stone wall in front of her as he thrust inside her. She squeezed her thighs around him tighter, wanting to give him as much pleasure as he'd given her.

"Yes, that's it," he groaned, and began to move. At first he could not go far, but they quickly established a rhythm of retreat and thrust, their movements perfectly matched, as if they had danced this dance many times before.

And yet as he moved behind her, his hands grasping her hips, she wished they were closer. She wanted to see his face, to understand what he felt, to know when he was about to come. She never tired of watching her lovers and had always enjoyed the physical closeness of sex as much as the other feelings it brought to her.

But as his breathing became more labored the tension within her began to build once more and once more she became focused within herself. The combination of the depth and angle of his thrusts was definitely rubbing her the right way. She arched slightly, wanting to take in more of him, her fingers digging into the stones in front of her. This was unlike any sex she'd had before. And perhaps that was one reason every sensation was so new and intense.

With a hard thrust, he drove her up against the wall, a sharp, guttural cry announcing his climax. The next thrust brought her to orgasm for the second time. A few more thrusts and they were both spent. He continued to hold on to her hips as he slid from her, then he bent and gathered her close, her back to his front, his face pressed against her shoulder, their pounding hearts gradually slowing, their breathing returned to normal.

Neither said anything until they'd pulled apart. He handed her the wet towel and she used it to clean herself, then she found her clothes and quickly dressed. Why she was so reluctant to stand before him naked puzzled her, but then, nothing about this encounter was usual for her.

"I guess it's a little late to ask now, but are you still on birth control?" he asked.

She blinked. Why hadn't *she* thought of that before now? She was usually so careful. In fact, she never had sex with a man for the first time without insisting he wear a condom. After they'd been seeing each other a while and she was convinced he was healthy, then she might agree to let him ride bareback, but this afternoon none of that had even entered her mind. "Yes, I'm still on the pill," she said. "And I don't have any diseases. What about you?"

"I already told you I'm practically a monk. You don't have anything to worry about."

"That's good, then."

He rubbed the back of his neck, avoiding her gaze. "I don't know about you, but that was pretty incredible just now," he said. "It's like..." He shook his head and tried again. "When I'm with you, it's almost like I'm a different person."

She nodded. "I know what you mean." Except she wasn't so sure she liked the person she became—that passive, needy woman who received attention but didn't play an active role in lovemaking.

He laughed nervously. "I've never had any complaints from women, but with you I feel like a superstud."

"Maybe you've been underestimating yourself before." In truth, she hadn't *needed* to do anything special or give Adam any directions. He seemed instinctively to know what to do to please her. It was amazing, really, especially for a man who claimed not to have had many lovers.

"It's stopped raining," he said.

For the first time she realized the storm had passed. Sun cast a rectangle of light through the doorway of the tower. Adam checked his watch. "It's after five. I guess we'd better get back to the bay before the others send out a search party."

"Will I see you again?" she asked. The question sounded foolish, considering they'd be working together all summer, living on a tiny island with only a dozen other people. "I mean, we'll do this again, won't we?" Honestly, why couldn't she just come out and ask him if he wanted to have sex again? What was wrong with her?

He nodded. "I hope so. Maybe I could come to your

place again. We'd have more privacy there." He grinned. "And a bed."

They started down the path to the beach. Neither spoke, though he put out a hand to steady her as she stepped over a fallen branch, and she put her hand to his back in a gesture of tenderness. As they neared the end of the path, he stopped. "What's wrong?" she asked.

He looked down at his feet, then up at her again. "I'd just as soon keep this a secret," he said. "I'm not ashamed of you or anything, but I think it would be easier on both of us if the others didn't know."

"It's a small island. Don't you think they'll figure it out sooner or later?"

"Maybe. But it's none of their business. This is just between the two of us."

"All right," she agreed, amused. Most men she knew were eager to brag about their conquests. Adam was definitely a puzzle. "It's kind of exciting, anyway, sneaking around," she added. "What do you want me to say if someone asks what we were doing together all afternoon?"

"Tell them we met up at the shower. They don't need to know anything else."

"Hmm, maybe next time we'll try out that shower together."

"Maybe so." He grinned. "One thing for sure, you're making this summer a lot more interesting than I expected."

"Oh, we haven't even started yet, Professor. I specialize in interesting." She cast a coquettish look over her shoulder, then sauntered past him onto the beach. She felt more like herself now, sexy and sassy, and walked with an exaggerated sway of her hips, knowing his gaze was fixed on her. Maybe all she'd needed to feel like herself again was a session of good, hot sex. Adam had provided that and then some.

5

ADAM HAD HEADED for the showers in a foul mood, annoyed at having to put off work at the *Eve* due to the inclement weather. But his encounter with Sandra had left him in much better spirits. While he still had no intention of getting seriously involved with the reporter, he could see that giving in to their obvious desire for each other wasn't weakness on his part, but practicality. Rather than waste so much energy brooding over her, he was now free to devote the bulk of his attention to the salvage operation. And after all, sex was a proven stress reliever. Right now he felt better than he had in months.

That euphoria lasted all the way back to his yacht. He climbed on deck, intending to fix himself a drink and spend the rest of the evening studying photographs of the wreck site and planning the next day's tasks. Thankfully, the weather had cleared, and tomorrow promised to be a good day. They'd get an early start and make up some of the time they had lost this afternoon.

But as soon as he set foot on the yacht, a man rose from a deck chair and greeted him. "Where have you been all afternoon?" the man asked in a peevish voice. "I've been waiting and waiting to talk to you."

Adam stared at his visitor. The last time he'd seen Damian Merrick, he'd been safely in Boston, where he was supposed to stay. "What are you doing here, Merrick?" he asked. "I thought we agreed your job was to provide the money for this expedition. My job was to do the actual recovery."

"I was in the area and thought I'd stop by and see if I couldn't help." Merrick glanced over his shoulder at a sleek racing yacht anchored a short distance away in the harbor. "After all, you don't have a very large crew. I'm glad to pitch in."

The last thing Adam needed was another amateur interfering or looking over his shoulder. But Merrick's millions were paying for the salvage of the *Eve* and as much as the man annoyed him, Adam couldn't afford to piss him off. "Thanks, but we've got everything under control."

He moved past the man toward the cabin. He needed that drink more than ever now.

Merrick grabbed Adam's arm as he passed. "Show me what you've found so far," he said, his expression as eager as a kid anticipating opening birthday presents. "Any gold? Jewels? Weapons?"

Adam had the dagger, the one he had wanted to show Sandra. Right now it rested in a fish bowl full of seawater in the galley. Artifacts that had been underwater for centuries had to be slowly leached of salt in order to prevent rapid decay when exposed to air. He wasn't inclined to show the dagger to Merrick, however. He didn't want to do anything that might encourage the man to hang around. "The best thing for you to do is to go back home or to wherever you were headed and not worry about us for the rest of the summer," he said. "When we find something of value, I'll be sure to let you know."

"Then you don't have anything to show me?" Merrick looked dismayed.

"We're still conducting the site survey," Adam said,

struggling to contain his irritation. "We're measuring and charting the area and taking photographs. I'm hoping to begin the actual salvage operations in a few days."

"All the more reason for me to stay around," Merrick said. "The work will go faster with an extra set of hands."

"That's very generous of you, but this is delicate, dangerous work. Someone with no training would be more of a hindrance than a help."

He started toward the cabin again, but Merrick came after him like one of those herding dogs who harry sheep about a pasture. "But I'm an excellent diver," he said. "I've dived wrecks before."

"Then you know it's tedious, dull work," Adam said. "I'm sure you have better things to do with your time."

"Honestly, I don't." Merrick beamed. "I don't have to be anywhere in particular for months and months."

Adam's stomach knotted. "You're determined to stay, then?"

Merrick's grin didn't waver. Dressed in a polo shirt, khaki shorts and well-worn topsiders, his light brown hair windblown and in need of a trim, he looked like the science nerd he was. All he needed was black-framed glasses and a pocket protector. "I won't be in the way, I promise. Think of me as another member of your crew."

A crew member who just happened to be worth several billion dollars. Adam swallowed the angry words that crowded at the back of his throat. He'd spent the better part of the past year writing letters, making phone calls and traveling back and forth across the country searching for someone with the money and the interest to finance the salvage of the *Eve*. Even a bare-bones recovery in shallow water such as he was proposing cost millions of dollars for supplies, equipment and personnel. Out of all the people he had contacted, Damian Merrick had been the one willing to write the checks. No matter how much he annoyed Adam, the success of the expedition ultimately depended on Merrick. Adam had no choice but to tolerate his presence.

"Be ready to head out at five-thirty in the morning," he said, then turned his back on the man and retreated to the cabin. He half expected Merrick to follow, but after a few moments he heard footsteps climbing down the ladder and the sound of a Zodiac motoring away. Adam poured a drink, his earlier ebullience vanished. Part of his excitement about this expedition had been the chance to lead the search and recovery of artifacts from the fabled pirate ship.

He was not a vain man or one who ordinarily craved fame, but the *Eve* had felt like his from the beginning. He was the only one searching for the ship, the one who found her, the one who had put so much effort into bringing her story to light. It grated to think he would now be forced to share the spotlight with the man who had bought and paid for that privilege. Adam had never had or aspired to have the kind of money Merrick possessed, but he would have given anything in this moment if he'd had the resources to tell Merrick to take a hike, and to keep the thrill of discovery all to himself.

SANDRA'S FIRST THOUGHT when she heard that Adam was beginning the next day's work at 5:30 a.m. was that he was trying to ditch her again. On further contemplation, she realized he was probably only trying to make up for time lost the day before. The man was clearly obsessed with this project. At least she could take credit for having his full attention for a brief time yesterday in the tower. Passionata had been right when she'd preached that few things could distract a man like sex.

Sandra was not a morning person, but she pushed herself to be at the wreck site by 6:00 a.m., ready to film. She was double-checking her air tanks, when an unfamiliar Zodiac motored alongside.

"Hello, I don't believe we've met," said a good-looking, dark-haired man in a turquoise-and-red wet suit. Two other men, whose attitude and dress clearly said flunky, manned the Zodiac and readied diving equipment. "I'm Damian Merrick. I'm going to be helping with the salvage operations."

Sandra recognized the name, if not the face. Damian Merrick's parents and grandparents had made fortunes in the steel and semiconductor industries, and Damian spent large chunks of that fortune backing various scientific and treasure-hunting endeavors, from a search for mythical Aztec gold to attempts to promote space travel for ordinary people. She'd heard Adam had persuaded the billionaire to agree to cough up some money to salvage the *Eve,* but she hadn't expected to meet Merrick himself.

Without waiting for an invitation, he boarded Sandra's craft and extended a hand. "You must be Ms. Newman. I've been looking forward to meeting you." There was nothing subtle about the way he checked her out, but neither was there anything particularly lascivious about his gaze. He had a boyish eagerness about him that some women probably found charming.

"Hello, Mr. Merrick," she said, continuing to check the gauges and meters on her diving gear. "I'm sorry I don't have a lot of time to visit, I've got work to do."

"I understand you're making a documentary about the project," he said, looming over her. "I've been studying the history of Passionata and the *Eve* and I'd be happy to talk to you about it."

"Hmm." It was too early in the morning to deal with

anyone, much less think of interviews. "My focus is really on the wreck itself," she said.

"We should have dinner sometime and talk. I'm sure the two of us have a lot in common."

In any other man, Sandra would have translated this to *I'm sure I can talk my way into your pants.* It was a familiar attitude, one she found comical or annoying, depending on the man and her mood. With Merrick, she couldn't be sure. Was he really as guileless and eager as he seemed?

In any case, she hadn't become as successful as she was by pissing off rich men. "I'm giving a party tomorrow night for everyone involved in the project," she said. "We can talk more then. Now I really do have to get down there."

"So do I." He hastened to help her lift the tanks into place. "I'm going to be diving as part of the crew."

She looked at him again. His wet suit looked brand-new and had obviously been expensive. His hair was carefully gelled and styled. He wore a gleaming chrome diving watch and a knife with a handle that looked like ivory. Definitely not the kind of gear sported by the average salvage crew. "Whose idea was that?" she asked. She'd bet half her salary it wasn't Adam's.

Merrick didn't take offense at the question. He grinned, showing dazzling white teeth. "I always like to keep an eye on my investments," he said.

She nodded and balanced on the edge of the Zodiac, preparing to go into the water. At her signal, Jonas flipped over the side ahead of her with his underwater video camera. She was hoping today to get some close-up views of the wreck. The idea was to give viewers a "before" look, a glimpse of what Adam had seen upon his first approach to the wreck last summer. "It was nice meeting you, Mr.

Merrick," she said. "I really have to go now." Not waiting for his answer, she let herself fall backward.

She quickly oriented herself and followed Jonas toward the wreck. A loud splash to her right startled her and she looked over to see Merrick coming after her. The man was persistent, she'd give him that.

Jonas slowed and pointed ahead, to a group of divers who hovered just above the ocean floor. One of the divers was operating a machine that blasted air across the floor, clearing away sediment, while two other divers, probably interns, took photographs and noted GPS coordinates. Sandra searched until she spotted Adam a little away from the group, studying something in his hand. The sight of him, in his plain black-and-gray wet suit, his blond hair a wild, wet mane around his face, made her smile. There was a power to Adam that had nothing to do with money or prestige. It was the strength of a man comfortable in himself, a strength she had felt yesterday afternoon in the tower.

Something pulling on her flipper distracted her. She looked around and saw Merrick had a hold of her. He pointed toward the group around the blower and gave her a questioning look. Did he really expect her to engage in a game of charades while they were underwater? She shook her head and pointed toward Jonas, who was busy filming the work. *Work.* What they were all here to accomplish. She kicked free of his hold and swam away, toward Adam.

The professor looked up at her approach. Just as well their diving gear made embracing awkward and kissing impossible, since he'd insisted on keeping their relationship a secret. She understood why he had done so, and even agreed, but after their encounter yesterday it was going to take a considerable amount of acting ability to pretend he was merely another man to her.

She pointed over her shoulder to Jonas and the camera. Merrick had abandoned her in favor of joining the group around the blower. She nodded toward him and gave Adam a questioning look.

The professor frowned, and he motioned Sandra closer. With their backs to Merrick and the others, Adam opened a pouch at his waist and removed a wrapped object. He handed it to her and indicated she should unwrap it. Curious, she did so.

She stared at the jeweled dagger which now lay in her hand, forgetting for a moment even to breathe. Even in this filtered light the dagger glowed, the delicate metal work around the jewels like fine lace. Her hand closed around it with the familiarity of habit, though she had never held a weapon like this before. The dizzy sensation she'd experienced in the upper tower room returned, and she closed her eyes, trying to steady herself.

An image flashed across her mind of a woman in a red brocade dress, her hair braided and piled upon her head beneath a headdress of gold and pearls. A young man knelt before her, his head bare, offering up the dagger. Sandra reached for the weapon as the woman reached for it, and with a start she realized they were one and the same. *She* was the woman in the brocade dress.

Adam's hand on her shoulder brought her back to her senses. Still clutching the dagger, she stared at him, fighting panic. What was happening to her? Was she losing her mind?

Adam leaned in close, both hands holding her now, his eyes full of concern. He reached over to check her gauges, and she felt a sense of relief. Maybe that was it—maybe something was wrong with her oxygen and that would explain the odd vision and dizziness. She needed to return to the surface at once and have her equipment checked out. Nodding to indicate she was okay, she pressed the dagger into his hands once more and pointed up over their heads. She even managed a smile.

He indicated he would follow her. She shook her head, but he insisted, and she didn't waste any more time trying to argue. But they rose only a few feet before they were intercepted by Merrick. He greeted them with a wave, then indicated the dagger and held out his hand to take it. Instead of giving it to him, Adam replaced the weapon in the pouch.

Merrick frowned and shook his head, but Adam ignored him. He took Sandra by the elbow, and they started up again, Merrick in their wake.

As soon as Adam broke through the surface, Merrick was at his side. "Was that a dagger you had?" he demanded. "Did you recover it from the shipwreck?"

"I don't have time to talk to you now," Adam said. "I have to take care of Sandra." He took Sandra's elbow and steered her toward the waiting Zodiac. "What happened down there?" he asked, trying to keep his voice low, so Merrick wouldn't hear. "You spaced out on me for a minute."

She shook her head. "It's nothing. I'm fine, really," she said. "I think I just…forgot to breathe or something."

He doubted holding one's breath would produce the dazed look that had come over her as she held the dagger— the same sort of look she'd had that night in her cabin, when she'd called him Frederick.

"Are you ill?" Merrick's attention switched to Sandra. "Let me help. I can take you back to my yacht and you can rest there."

Adam scowled at the man. Anyone who saw the way he

practically salivated over Sandra would know that *resting* was not what he had in mind. "She has a yacht of her own," he said. "She doesn't need yours."

"I'm *fine*, really." She waved them both away, as if she were swatting flies. "I'll switch out tanks and check all my equipment and get back down right away."

Her steward, Rodrigo, leaned down to help her into the Zodiac, and Adam prepared to boost her from behind, but he was suddenly shoved out of the way as Merrick swept in and practically *tossed* her into the boat.

She scrambled around and glared at them both, face flushed with anger. Adam put up both his hands. "I never touched you," he said.

"Sorry if I got a little carried away," Merrick said. "I was only trying to help."

It was just as well he'd already put the dagger away, Adam thought, or he'd be tempted to use it on the rich blowhard.

"Go away," Sandra said. "Both of you." She turned and nodded to Rodrigo and he revved the Zodiac's motor, leaving the two men bobbing in its wake.

Merrick grinned. "She's as feisty in person as she is on television, isn't she?" he said.

"If you call her feisty she's liable to scratch your eyes out," Adam said. Small dogs were feisty. Heroines in Broadway musicals were feisty. Sandra was bold, strong, sensuous and smart—but she was not feisty.

"She's probably bored," Merrick said. "Back in the States she's always making the gossip rags, photographed with this celebrity and that movie star. No one on this island is in her league."

"No, none of us are in that league," Adam said through clenched teeth. He knew a lowly history professor was not the type who normally interested a woman like Sandra—

further proof that her involvement with him here was merely a matter of expediency.

Though considering the heat the two of them had generated, he was doubtful a man would survive if she was *truly* interested in him.

"Tell me about this dagger," Merrick said. "Is it from the *Eve?*"

"Yes, it's from the wreck." Reluctantly, he took the dagger from the pouch. It wasn't as if Merrick wouldn't see it sooner or later, though Adam resented the man forcing himself into the project.

Merrick turned the dagger over and over in his hand. "Very pretty," he said. "But I don't think it's all that valuable."

"It's a beautiful piece." Adam snatched the dagger from Merrick and stowed it in the pouch once more. "A historically significant find."

"Maybe so, but I'm more interested in more valuable items. The real eye candy like jewels and gold." He glanced in the direction Sandra's Zodiac had departed. "It's what Sandra wants, too," he added. "Her viewers don't care about daggers."

As if this joker knew what Sandra wanted or didn't want. "I'll find your treasure," Adam said. "If you leave me alone to do it." With that, he shoved his mask over his eyes and dived, away from meddling millionaires, dazed TV divas and everything but the wreck that had been his obsession, his fantasy and his dream for years—the one place where he felt truly in charge.

6

SANDRA WAS MORE SHAKEN by her experience with the dagger than she would admit to Adam or Merrick. As soon as she reached the safety of the Zodiac, all she wanted was to be alone on her yacht, so she'd asked Rodrigo to take her there. Jonas and Albert could handle the filming by themselves this morning. She'd spend the hours before lunch trying to pull herself together enough to go out again.

The thought of something like that happening again while she was diving frightened her. What if she forgot herself completely and ripped out her regulator? What if she lost track of time and ran out of oxygen?

She poured a cup of tea, her hands shaking so badly the spout of the teapot rattled against the cup. *Get a grip,* she scolded herself. She was a professional and she had a job to do. She had to get past this silly fear.

Maybe stress had something to do with these momentary space outs. Pretty much everything was caused by stress these days. And she *was* tense, anxious to prove to her producer that he hadn't wasted his money, that she still had what it took to pull in an audience.

Fine. She could deal with stress. She'd taken yoga classes, practiced deep breathing and played around a little with meditation. Now that she'd identified the problem, she had the tools to handle it. And she'd start right now.

She set aside the tea and walked into the bedroom, where she lay down on the bed. Arms at her sides, she closed her eyes and focused on her breathing. Deep breath in…one, two, three, four. Exhale slowly…four, three, two, one. Clear her mind. Relax. Let all the stress go. She was perfectly calm. At peace. No worries at all….

She didn't realize how tired she was until she relaxed. She fought sleep for a few moments, then surrendered to its embrace.

SHE AWOKE to a darkened room, nothing visible beyond the draperies that hung around her bed. She was instantly alert, tense, aware of another's presence nearby. She could hear someone breathing, slowly and evenly, moving toward her.

The curtains parted and a man's silhouette loomed over her. "Hello, my dear," he said. "I apologize for keeping you waiting."

"Hello, Frederick." The words came automatically, with no conscious thought. She stared at him, trying to make out his features, but they were obscured in the darkness.

He knelt on the bed and lit a candle on a low table beside them. The feeble flame revealed that he was naked, the corded muscle of his arms and shoulders and the washboard line of his abdomen burnished gold. She squeezed her thighs together against a sharp, hot wave of desire.

When he grasped the silken gown she wore and slid it from her shoulder, she didn't protest, but leaned toward him, craving his touch. He was a stranger to her mind, but to her body he was more familiar than her own reflection, the man who had taught her about sex, the only man she had truly been with, the one without whom she felt incomplete.

"I want to do something special tonight," he said as he bared her breasts, his face still in shadow. His voice was low and rough, velvet over jagged stone, every syllable sending a hot shiver pulsing through her.

"Wh-what is that?" she asked. She felt jumpy and anxious, every nerve raw with wanting, as if she'd been waiting on him for hours instead of mere seconds.

"Close your eyes," he said.

She immediately did as he asked, even as part of her brain protested that she wasn't the type to act without knowing the reasons why. Still, her eyes remained firmly shut, her ears straining to decipher the sounds of his movements.

Something cool and silky glided across her face, smelling of tobacco and rich perfume. She opened her mouth to speak and felt the drag of fabric across her tongue. "Should I use this as a gag, to muffle your screams of pleasure when I make you come?" he asked.

Her stomach recoiled in fear at the idea of being gagged, even as the reminder that he could make her scream in pleasure set up a throbbing between her legs. She started to open her eyes, in hopes of at last seeing his face and reading the expression there, but the cloth came up to block her vision, the folds soft against her eyelids.

"Yes, this is what I want," he said as he knotted the scarf behind her head. He smoothed her hair beneath the cloth, then rested his hand upon her head, the weight of it pressing her down into the mattress. "I want you to experience our lovemaking with all your other senses," he said. "To feel the heat of me inside you, the sensation of skin on skin, the tightening of muscle as you near your peak."

"Yes." His words left her breathless, mesmerized. He had scarcely touched her and already she was primed for him.

She reached for him, but he gently pushed her hands away. The mattress beside her dipped from his weight. "Relax, and tell me what you feel," he said.

The bed creaked as his weight shifted again. His hands grasped her legs, pushing them apart. Cool air rushed across her thighs, then a sensation like ice trailing from her knee to the juncture of her legs. "It's cold…and wet," she said, arching toward his touch, heat pooling in her abdomen.

But he skipped over her aching sex, trailing chilled liquid across her stomach and down her other thigh. "What is it?" she asked.

"Taste." Something nudged her lips, and tart liquid trickled over her tongue. She savored the taste of wine, suddenly parched. It was as if every appetite was suddenly made keener—hunger and thirst and desire coalescing into one great need.

She protested as the wine was withdrawn, but her objection turned to a cry of delight as his lips closed over her thigh. He followed the path he had laid down with the wine, lips and tongue teasing sensitive nerves until she trembled and moaned.

"Tell me how much you want me," he said.

"I want you so much," she gasped.

"How much?"

"So much…if I don't have you, I'm afraid I might die."

He cupped his hand over her mons. "You won't die. And I don't believe you want me enough. Not yet."

"I do!" she insisted, frustration mounting. She reached for him, but he grabbed her wrists and held them.

"Desire is not just physical, *ma chère,*" he said. "For true ecstasy to be reached, one must engage both the body and the mind. I know I have aroused your body. Now my task is to excite your mind." He traced the side of her cheek with one finger, then kissed her forehead gently.

She struggled to breathe easier, to contain the feeling of

powerlessness that both frustrated and excited her. Depending on someone else for her pleasure felt both confining and freeing. If nothing was expected of her, then she was free to enjoy all. She focused on this, her attention on the desire that hummed through her like a current, telling herself not to anticipate but to accept, to experience to the fullest whatever was offered.

His mouth closed around her breast, sending a jolt of sensation through her. She clawed at the bedding, gripping the sheets, holding on as if she might suddenly fly off. With only blackness before her eyes, every movement came as a surprise, every sensation intensified.

His mouth still at her breasts, he inserted two fingers into her vagina, thrusting deep, making her gasp and bow her back. "Yes," she hissed through clenched teeth, her clit throbbing against the heel of his hand.

As soon as she said the word he withdrew. "Not yet," he said, and she hated his cruelty even as she craved the return of his touch.

With his mouth and tongue he painted a path down her torso, circling her navel, charting a course down her thighs. She arched toward him in blatant invitation. A voice inside her head urged her to sit up, rip off the blindfold, push him down on the bed and demand he satisfy her. In her experience, that kind of thing was as much of a turn-on for men as it was for her—at least, it was for the kind of men she preferred to hang out with.

But that voice was drowned out by the urge to remain passive, to wait for him to satisfy her at his leisure.

He moved away, and she feared he had left her altogether. She rose up on her elbows and was reaching for the scarf when one hand on her shoulder pushed her back again. "Only a little longer now," he said.

She gasped as chilled liquid bathed her clit, the rush of sensation bringing her to the very edge. Then his mouth closed over her, drinking the wine, lapping and suckling with a fervor that erased all coherent thought. She gave herself up to this joyous release, shouting her pleasure as wave after wave of climaxes rolled over her.

Then he knelt over her, hands pushing her thighs wide apart as he buried himself in her. She tightened around him, clinging as he withdrew, rising to receive him once more. As he thrust into her again and again, she had a sudden recollection of another time, her palms pressed against rough stones, her lover's face hidden from her, each movement sending her spiraling upward toward a second release. This moment had the same intensity, the same feeling of losing control, the same regret that she couldn't look into her partner's eyes, to see the transformation at the moment of his release, to read in his eyes his true feelings for her.

And then he was done, pulling out of her, leaving her wanting more. "Wait," she called, but he was already across the room, the door closing softly behind him.

"Wait," she said again, to the empty room.

Then the candle sputtered, faltered and went out, plunging the room into darkness. Dizziness assailed her again and she fell back against the pillows, closed her eyes and slipped once more into oblivion.

AFTER SANDRA LEFT, Adam focused on completing the survey of the east side of the wreck. The new magnetometer had arrived on schedule and it showed a lot of promising deposits on that side, which could be anything from silver ingots to iron bolts. He had Charlie and Brent blowing sand from these locations, taking photographs and making notes while Adam considered the best way to salvage and preserve whatever they found.

Unfortunately, Merrick insisted on dogging Adam's every step, like a trailing barracuda—mostly harmless but annoying, and a hazard around which Adam couldn't afford to let down his guard.

Adam tried to ignore Merrick and to put aside his worries about Sandra. Her sudden departure from the wreck site worried him. There must be more to her odd behavior when he'd shown her the dagger than she'd let on.

When the crew broke for lunch, Adam found Jonas and asked him about Sandra. "She said she wasn't feeling well," the cameraman said. "I figured maybe it was some female problem."

"Uh, right." Adam backed away. Maybe Sandra just had cramps or something and would be fine in a day or two. In any case, it was really none of his business. Having sex with her didn't make him responsible for her.

Adam had taken three bites from his sandwich when Merrick loomed over him. The billionaire had shed his wet suit and wore baggy black trunks. "When are we going to be done with all these photographs and surveys and start the real salvage work?" he asked.

Adam took his time chewing. When he'd finally swallowed, he said, "Do you think I should go down there and scoop up everything in sight as quickly as possible?"

"Exactly." Merrick sat beside him. "The less time this takes, the sooner we'll get to all the treasure."

Adam scowled at him. "Some treasure hunters do things that way, but I'm not one of them. I'm a historian. Knowing where items are found, their relationship to each other and possibly how they got there is as important as the items themselves," he said.

Merrick frowned. "Well, sure, the history is important, but aren't you anxious to find out what's down there? Isn't there any way to speed things up?"

Adam fixed Merrick with an even look. "There's a right way to do these things and a wrong way. Doing things the wrong way endangers the people I'm working with. It can also compromise the value of the treasure."

Merrick laughed. "The average collector doesn't care whether a gold bar was found in the front of the ship or the back, or ten feet away on the ocean floor," he said.

"You're right," Adam said. "But I also know collectors want items that are in as mint condition as possible. If we start hacking around with shovels and indiscriminately scooping up items, there's a very good chance we'll nick or scar them, which could seriously detract from their value."

Merrick considered this, then nodded. "I see what you're saying, but that takes us back to my original question. How much longer are you going to spend on pictures and surveys? When are you going to actually start retrieving stuff?"

Adam crushed his napkin in his fist and stood. Merrick was taller, but Adam probably outweighed him by thirty pounds, and none of that weight was fat. "We'll do it when I'm ready," he said. Not waiting for an answer, he pushed past the billionaire and moved toward the other end of the boat.

Merrick followed. "Let me help you. It will speed things up."

"Absolutely not."

"Why not? I told you, I've dived wrecks before."

"Professionally or as a tourist?"

"Not professionally, but—"

"Then you've dived wrecks that hundreds of other

divers have visited." Adam knelt and began checking gauges on compressed air tanks. "Stable wrecks with marked or known hazards. Ones left in place specifically for amateurs—tourists."

Merrick put his hands on his hips. "There must be something I can do."

You can get the hell away from me and leave me to work in peace, Adam thought. But if Merrick was so eager to help, he could certainly put him to work. "You can help Charlie and Brent. They'll show you what to do."

At last, Merrick left him alone. The next time Adam saw him, he was with Brent and Charlie, listening intently as they explained the equipment they were using.

Tessa dived with Adam that afternoon. They ran the magnetometer over a gridded section of the debris field. His search this morning had uncovered only bits of rusted iron from the ship—keel bolts and hinges, the wheels from an artillery cassion, but no actual guns.

They had similar results this afternoon, with the added excitement of unearthing a single cannonball, its surface pitted with rust and home to a spiny sea urchin.

They had been down thirty minutes when they headed to the surface. Charlie and Brent joined them on the dive boat as they were removing their tanks. "We've covered everything in our grid," Brent announced.

Adam nodded. "Us, too. I think tomorrow we can start excavation."

"Hot damn! That's what I've been waiting to hear." Charlie grinned.

"Do you think there's any real treasure?" Tessa asked. "Gold and silver and stuff like that?"

Adam nodded. "I think there's a good chance. The *Eve* was reportedly returning from a productive raid on a

Spanish merchant fleet when she was sunk." The more he talked about the possibilities that lay on the ocean floor, the more excited he was about tomorrow's dive. His only regret was that he would have to share the glory of discovery with Merrick, who would insist on being a part of everything.

Speaking of the wealthy thorn in his side… "Where's Merrick?" he asked, looking around.

Charlie shrugged. "How should I know?"

Adam's stomach knotted. "Wasn't he working with you two?"

Brent shook his head. "He asked us a bunch of stuff about what we were doing, but as soon as we dove, he headed off toward you. I thought he was working with you, the same as this morning."

Merrick hadn't been *working* with Adam that morning, but there was no sense pointing that out now. "Which way did he head, *exactly?*" he asked.

Brent and Charlie looked at each other. "Toward the other side of the canyon," Brent said. "You and Tessa were working over there. Didn't you see him?"

"Damn!" Adam punched the side of the boat in frustration.

"What's wrong?" Tessa asked.

"Merrick's decided to go exploring on his own. At lunch he was trying to convince me to let him go, and I refused. I told him it was too dangerous. So he agreed to work with you two instead." Adam shook his head. "I should have known he was up to something when he gave in so easily."

"He's been down there a long time by himself," Tessa said.

"That was stupid," Brent said. "What if he's hurt or something?"

"I'm more concerned he's wrecking the grids we've already laid down." Adam began pulling on his equipment again. "Charlie, find a couple of fresh tanks and come with me. Brent, you and Tessa be ready to dive if we need more help." He silently cursed Merrick and his arrogance. Obviously having a lot of money didn't guarantee a man had any common sense. Or any respect for the work they'd already done.

Whatever he was up to, Adam would make him live to regret it. There would be only one boss on this expedition, and it wasn't Merrick.

7

WHEN SANDRA WOKE, afternoon sun poured into the room through the single porthole. She blinked up at the white ceiling, confused by a memory of red curtains surrounding the bed. What had happened to them? She turned to glance at the bedside table and saw only a lamp and the novel she had been reading. No candle. No silk scarf to serve as a blindfold. No open bottle of wine.

She ran her hands down her body, her thumbs catching on the metallic decorations of her bikini. What had happened to the long silk gown she remembered?

Remembered? Or imagined?

Feeling sick to her stomach, she replayed the encounter with the faceless lover. A new wave of sickness swept over her as she remembered addressing him as Frederick.

"Who the hell is Frederick?" she asked, sitting up.

But of course, no one answered.

She covered her eyes with one hand. It wasn't enough that she was hallucinating; now she was reduced to talking to herself.

She got out of bed and went into the bathroom where she ran cold water over her wrists, then brushed her teeth, staring into the mirror. She looked the same as she always did, except perhaps for the haunted look in her eyes. Well, who wouldn't look a little upset if she thought she was going crazy?

She pulled on a pair of shorts and a shirt, and began to pace. She always thought better on her feet, and there had to be a logical explanation for this. First of all, who was Frederick? And how could she find out if she never saw his face?

Of course, there were other ways of identifying a man, and she'd seen plenty of Frederick to recognize him again. The thing was, he'd never felt completely like a stranger to her. If he was a product of her imagination, she'd created him from familiar parts.

Parts that in this case belonged to a particular history professor. She stopped in the middle of the room and hugged her arms across her stomach, adding up all the connections between Adam and Frederick: they both had blond hair. They both were big, muscular men. They both were very good in the sack.

Right. And all that proved was that she had a very good imagination. Under other circumstances, what woman wouldn't welcome dreams that were so vivid they gave her orgasms? Think of the possibilities—all the pleasure of sex with a man with none of the messy relationship details to worry about. No possibility of getting pregnant or contracting some sexually transmitted disease.

Also none of the closeness her dreams had left her craving. Then again, her most recent encounter with Adam had left her craving that, too.

It didn't matter how pleasurable the dreams were, they freaked her out. They weren't just happening at night, and they were interfering with her life. With her work. There had to be something causing them—some malfunction with her diving equipment, or something she'd eaten or had to drink. She stopped pacing and headed for the desk in the other room, where she knew she had a pad of paper and pens. She'd write down everything she'd put into her mouth since that first dinner with Adam....

Adam. He'd been with her—or nearby—every time she'd had one of these crazy spells. He hadn't been in her cabin that afternoon, but she'd been standing right next to him when she'd spaced out in the water, he'd been in her cabin when she'd had her first episode, and he claimed to have been taking a shower next to the tower when she'd hallucinated in the upper room.

Could Adam somehow be *causing* her strange dreams and delusions? But how? He had no reason to want to harm her. They got along well together—especially in bed.

No, Adam couldn't be responsible. But he might be the one person who could help. She couldn't continue to battle this on her own.

Agitation compelled her to pace again. She'd have to confront Adam privately. She'd have to trust him enough to confide in him and ask for his help, and she didn't want to do that in front of an audience.

Would he help her? They'd agreed to a relationship based on casual sex. Now that she needed more from him, would he balk? Could she compete with his admitted obsession with a shipwreck and the history of a long-dead pirate queen?

Passionata. That was it. The key to gaining the interest of Adam—or of any man—was to follow the example of Passionata. Tomorrow night, during the big beach party she'd offered to throw for everyone, she'd lure Adam away from the others on the pretense of a repeat of their fun at the tower. Then she'd ask for his help in figuring out what was wrong with her. If she played her part well, there'd be no way he could refuse her.

As ADAM LED the rescue party toward the *Eve,* he tried to plot a strategy for dealing with Merrick. There was always the possibility he wasn't snooping where he didn't belong, but instead was injured or ill. Charlie and Adam both carried supplemental oxygen and spare regulators, as well as basic first-aid gear. They could get Merrick back to the ship, but they didn't have the facilities to deal with a serious injury.

Damn the man! He'd been nothing but trouble since he'd shown up on the island.

The debris field that marked the shipwreck site lay ahead of them, awash in bright colors as if someone had used it for paintball practice: red, orange and yellow anemones, shiny black sea urchins, green sponges, blue and purple sea cucumbers and white coral all lurked beneath the orange-and-white grid the team had laid down. Dark shadows glided among the busted casks and other relics that littered the area—toothy barracudas, serpentine eels and stealthy black-tipped sharks.

Adam played the handheld spotlight over the area. He glimpsed movement out of the corner of his eye and swung the light around to fix on a lone diver.

Merrick was kneeling on top of the grid, scooping out the sand within and tossing it aside. Anger surged through Adam at the sight of such carelessness. Along with all that sand, Merrick might be tossing away fragments of glass, bullets, pottery or other artifacts. Switching off the light, he swam toward the interloper, Charlie close behind.

Adam had grabbed Merrick and pinioned his arms behind him by the time Charlie reached them. The younger man tried to pull Adam away, but Adam shrugged him off. He glared at Merrick, who stared back with aggravating calm. Adam indicated Charlie should take Merrick's other arm and together they hauled him toward the surface, pausing halfway up to rest and acclimate. At that point, Merrick pulled away from them, though he made no attempt to swim away. He ignored Adam's murderous looks, smiling and patting the neoprene bag at his waist, which bulged suspiciously. Adam crossed his arms over his chest, fighting the almost overwhelming urge to attack the man.

Up top, Merrick preceded them into the dive boat, where Brent collected his air tanks. "You're almost out of air," he said after checking the gauges.

Merrick shrugged. "I knew I had enough to make it back up."

Adam grabbed his arm and turned him around. "What do you think you were doing?" he demanded. "I told you not to interfere with our work."

"I knew there was treasure down there," he said. "I didn't see any harm in going after it myself. Just to get a taste of what's in store for us."

"You didn't see any harm, did you?" Adam roared.

Merrick made a face. "I was *tired* of waiting."

"I don't care what you're tired of," Adam said, clenching and unclenching his fists at his sides. Some shred of willpower kept him from decking the billionaire, but that shred was growing thinner by the second. "I'm in charge of this expedition. *I* say when excavation begins. What you did could have jeopardized our research. And you may have unknowingly destroyed other artifacts."

"I didn't destroy these." Merrick pulled the bag from his waist and upended it on the deck in front of them. A shower of gold spilled out, hitting the deck with heavy metallic thunks, gleaming in the bright sun.

Adam leaned down and picked up what proved to be a

gold coin—a Spanish eight *escudo* piece, more commonly known as a doubloon.

"Worth $1500 to $2000 on today's market," Merrick said.

Adam looked down at his feet again; he counted seven additional doubloons lying there. "There are more where those came from, I'm sure," Merrick said.

Find enough of these and Adam would never again have to worry about having the funds to indulge any interest he desired. Locate a chest full of these and Sandra's viewers would "ooh" and "ahh" and talk about it for days. If the wreck indeed held more such coins, none of them would have to worry about doubters ever again.

"Now we know there's something down there worth hunting for," Merrick said. He snatched the doubloon away from Adam and started to pocket it, but Roger's hand was quicker.

"I'll take that," the older man said. He bent and scooped up the others, as well. "These will need to be conserved, cataloged and placed with the rest of the artifacts."

"I found those," Merrick protested. "They should belong to me."

"You're part of the team, remember?" Adam said. "All the items recovered stay together until they're divided up to be sold or distributed to museums and research facilities." He looked Merrick in the eye. "Your money got you here, but it doesn't give you any special privileges. From now on you do as I say, just like everyone else. You'll work with one of us and anything you find gets turned over to me."

Merrick stuck his lower lip out in a pout. "And if I don't want to abide by your rules?"

"Take your money and go home." Adam turned away. "I'll find other financing." He had the money from Sandra's network to tide him over. Those eight doubloons, and the photos he'd taken already, would go a long way toward helping him get the rest.

"All right." Merrick's voice was loud and clear behind him. "I'll do it. I'll work as one of the team."

Adam faced him once more. "You'll do as I say?"

He hesitated, then nodded. "Consider me one of your humble crew." His mouth twitched, as if he was trying not to smile.

That smile defused the last of Adam's anger. Merrick was as far from humble as a person could be, but he apparently wanted to be a part of this expedition badly enough to try to fake humility, at least for a while. He was a decent diver, strong enough to be a real help. Adam stuck out his hand. "All right then. Welcome aboard."

Merrick's handshake was firm and steady. "Glad to be here, Professor. I thought for a minute there you were going to make me walk the plank."

"Next time I just might." He'd been angry enough at Merrick to think himself capable of anything. Time on the island was revealing all sorts of hidden character traits, from the great passion Sandra brought out in him, to the potential for savagery worthy of any pirate.

"I WISH I'D HAD A CAMERA to take a picture of the professor's face when he saw all that gold." Merrick raised his gin and tonic in Adam's direction. "It was the first time I've ever seen him at a loss for words."

"I couldn't believe you'd take that kind of risk for something we would have found eventually, anyway," Adam said. Everyone was gathered on the beach for Sandra's party, and Adam was on his second beer, but it hadn't yet erased the scowl he'd worn ever since Merrick had begun pontificating on their afternoon's adventure.

Sandra could admit to a stab of jealousy over Merrick being the one to discover the first real treasure of the *Eve*— at a time when she hadn't been around to film it.

"You exaggerate the risk," Merrick said. "When you found me, I was fine, and about to return to the surface on my own." He winked at Sandra. "It's too bad you weren't there. You could have filmed the dramatic discovery for your documentary."

"Yes, I'm sorry I missed it."

"You look like you're feeling better now," Adam said to her, not even attempting to be subtle about his desire to shift attention away from Merrick.

"Much better, thank you." She smoothed her hands across the short silk sarong she wore. The lightweight fabric clung to her curves, and the bright blue and yellow color set off her hair and eyes. She'd gone to some trouble to look especially appealing tonight. Judging by the way neither man could keep his eyes off her, she'd succeeded.

She poured herself a drink from the makeshift bar that had been set up on the edge of the sand and surveyed the festivities. "It's turned out to be quite a nice party," she observed. Everyone involved in the salvage project had been invited and had gathered to savor fried grouper, steamed mussels, grilled hamburgers, roasted corn and a tower of brownies the cook on the *Caspian* had presented to cheers and applause. Beer, wine and mixed drinks were available, and a large bonfire cast a bright glow over all.

"Yes," Adam said. "It's good for everyone to relax and get to know one another better before the really hard work begins."

"You've already been working hard," she said. "You mean, it gets worse?"

"We're probably going to have to shift a lot of sand and

heavy beams and other wreckage to get down to the level where the contents of the ship's hold most likely settled. And once storm season heats up, we have to make the most of every day of good weather. That means long hours." His eyes met hers. "Hunting for treasure isn't as glamorous as most people seem to think."

"All the more reason for us to make the most of whatever time we have together now," she murmured. She looked into his eyes, feeling the familiar surge of arousal he so often called forth. He fascinated her, frustrated and confused her, and when she was with him, her emotions were in a constant turmoil. He couldn't be good for her, but she couldn't stay away from him.

Which meant she'd have to be extra vigilant to remain on task this evening. She wanted his body, yes. But she wanted his help more.

WHEN ADAM'S EYES MET Sandra's, she immediately had his full attention. One look from her and his cock was hard. He glanced toward the bonfire, where the others sat, enthralled by some story Roger was relating about a dive he'd made off the coast of Africa. Adam pulled Sandra into the welcoming shadows.

As soon as they were hidden from the others, she draped herself around him, her lips locked to his in a kiss that made him forget everything short of his own name. His hands slid down her back to cradle her bottom, and he pulled her closer still, until she was riding his thigh. "I've missed you," she said.

"I've missed you, too." He nudged his erection against her so she could feel how much.

"Let's go to your yacht, where we can be alone," she said in a low, husky voice that made him think of smoky bars, black-and-white movies and forbidden liaisons.

Loud laughter came from the party behind them, and the bonfire leaped to new heights as someone added another armful of driftwood to the blaze. Someone else turned up the boombox as a steel drum tune played. He took her hand and silently led her down the beach toward his yacht to explore a different world—one of shadows and secrets and sex.

8

ADAM HAD A NICE VIEW of Sandra's ass as she climbed the ladder to his yacht. He'd left a lantern burning to light his way back, and in its glow he noticed that, though the leopard-print silk skirt clung tightly to her bottom, there were no panty lines. Did that mean she wasn't wearing any panties? The thought made it necessary for him to stop and adjust his shorts.

On board she took a seat on a lounger. "Do you have any wine?" she asked.

He would have just as soon skipped the drink and picked up where they'd left off on the beach, but he played along and fetched a bottle of *prosecco* from the galley and opened it.

He handed her a half-full glass and sat on the end of the lounger. "I had a dream this afternoon," she said. "About you. At least I think it was you."

"You don't know?"

"I never saw my dream man's face, but his body was definitely familiar." She leaned over and ran one hand across his shoulder and squeezed his arm.

He sipped his wine, still playing it cool. This was a kind of foreplay, too, sitting close and not touching, every look and gesture speaking of desire as yet unfulfilled. "Tell me about this dream," he said.

"We had wine, and you poured it on me and licked it off."

"Like this?" He leaned forward and dripped wine into her cleavage, then dove for it with his tongue.

The heat of her skin quickly warmed the liquid, intensifying the flavor. He traced the swell of the top of her breast with his tongue and felt her shiver beneath him. Some of the wine trickled into the fabric of her dress, and he sucked it from the cloth, her nipples hardening at the touch of his mouth.

She arched against him, her responsiveness making him more eager than ever. "Why is it I'm so impatient with you?" he asked.

"Are you impatient?" She pushed him away and leaned back to study him.

"Yes." He drained the wineglass and set it aside on the deck. "I can't stop thinking about you, and when I'm with you, I want you immediately, if not sooner."

She smiled, a look as seductive as any he'd seen. "How much do you want me?" she asked.

"This much." He pushed her back and straddled her, his cock pressed tight to her clit. He rocked back and forth, stroking her through the layers of clothing. "I fantasize about taking you twice," he said. "Once quick and hard just to satisfy this urgency in me, then again, long and slow, building to a climax that leaves us both half out of our senses."

Her eyes widened. "I had no idea a history professor could be so sensual."

"This history professor isn't, usually. But you bring out that side of me."

She reached down and stroked the fly of his shorts. "The first time hard and fast, you said. Would you make me scream?"

"Yes. I want to hear you scream." He pulled up her skirt. As he'd suspected, she was naked beneath the thin silk. He stroked her clit, then sank his fingers into her hot, moist passage. She closed tightly around him. "You're wet," he said, rasping out the words. "Maybe you want it fast, too."

Her eyes had a glazed look and she struggled to focus on him once more. "Yes. But I want to be on top."

He rolled over and slid under her, helping her to position herself over him. She unzipped his shorts and he slid them to his ankles, then kicked them off.

She wrapped her hand around him and squeezed gently, sending a jolt of desire through him. "Are you always this horny?" she asked.

"Only around you."

"What is it about me, you think, that turns you on so much?"

"I don't know," he said honestly, wishing she wasn't so interested in talking. He was all for communication, but couldn't they have this discussion later?

"But what do you think?" she asked.

He sighed. "I've tried to figure that out. You're not the type I usually go for."

She grinned. "Too high maintenance?"

He hesitated. "Yes, I think that's part of it. But I doubt I'm the type of man you usually date."

"That's true."

"In fact, I think Damian Merrick is more your type."

"Rich and nerdy?" She began to slide her hand up and down his cock, making it difficult for him to think. "I'm sorry you have such a poor opinion of me," she said.

"Right now I think you're the most wonderful woman I ever met, and if you keep stroking my cock that way, I'm going to think you're even more wonderful."

"Point taken." She slid down his body and took him in

her mouth. He arched off the chaise, her tongue and lips doing an erotic dance across his swollen flesh, rendering him incoherent.

She moved to his balls, her tongue tickling over them, then taking him in her mouth, applying gentle suction. He groaned, eyes closed, head back, anticipating fast-approaching bliss.

She moved away, up his body to his chest, where she began to lick and suckle his nipples. His erection strained against her thigh, and he wondered if he'd embarrass himself by coming before he was even in her.

She stripped off the dress and tossed it aside, the breeze catching it and sending it scudding across the deck to land against the starboard rail. She straddled him, her sex pressed against his stomach, hot and moist. She ran her hands over her breasts, cradling them, stroking them, plucking at the nipples. "Are you ready to take me now?" she asked.

In answer, he reached for her and tried to pull her to him, but she resisted. "Not yet," she said, leaning back. "I have a few questions for you first."

"Questions?" He blinked at her. *"Now?"*

"Yes." She braced both hands on his chest. "I need some help from you, and I don't intend to let you up until you tell me what I want to know."

"I'll tell you anything if I can do it while my cock's inside of you."

Her lips curved in a half smile. "That's exactly what I was counting on."

SANDRA HAD ADAM exactly where she wanted him. Or rather—she *wanted* him, but first she needed to find out if he knew anything about her crazy hallucinations and realistic sexual fantasies. If she could only keep her hormones in check long enough to question him—not easy to accomplish with his erection nudging at her entrance, promising ecstasy if she'd only let him in.

He arched beneath her. "Come on, Sandra," he said. "Enough with the games. You're driving me crazy, here."

Crazy. That was the magic word all right. She slid off of him and stood a safe distance away, resisting the urge to wrap her dress around her body once more. She wanted to talk to Adam without his quick temper and impatience getting in the way. Questioning him naked seemed a good way to meet that goal. "Where were you this afternoon after I left the wreck site?" she asked.

He sat up and swung his feet over the edge of the lounger. "What do you mean, where was I? I was at the wreck, completing our survey. And then I was looking for Merrick."

"So you didn't leave the wreck site at all?"

"No." He frowned. "What would I have been doing instead?"

"You didn't come to my cabin and have sex with me?"

He looked truly confused; either he was an amazing actor, a pathological liar or he was telling the truth. "I don't know what you're talking about. Was someone in your cabin this afternoon?"

"I don't know." She knotted her hands in fists at her sides and began to pace, all thoughts of seduction abandoned. "Something is happening to me, and it seems to have something to do with you."

"Me?" He stood. "Are you talking about these weird spells you've been having? You think I'm responsible for those?"

"They only happen when you're around," she said. "I'm either with you, or you show up soon afterward."

He took her by the shoulders and guided her back to the chaise. "Sit down and tell me exactly what's happening," he said. "I promise I'm not responsible, but maybe I can help you figure things out."

He sounded so calm. So reasonable. So understanding. More willing to help than she'd expected. It took everything in her to keep from throwing herself into his arms and sobbing with both fear and relief. But she was made of stronger stuff than that, so she took a deep breath, pulled herself together and told him about the odd sensations she'd had with him at dinner on her yacht, in the tower both before and after he joined her there, in the ocean with the dagger and later in her cabin.

"And you think I'm doing something to cause all this?" he asked when she was done.

"What else am I supposed to think? Nothing like this has ever happened to me before."

"But what do you think I did? I already told you I didn't put anything in the food or drink we shared in your cabin. And I was in the shower when you hallucinated in the tower, and at the wreck site this morning."

"I don't know. I believe that you wouldn't intentionally harm me." She squeezed her hands together, trying to control her turbulent emotions. "I was hoping, since you were there, that you'd seen something or noticed something or someone—"

"But who would want to harm you?" he asked.

"I don't know!"

He put his arm around her and patted her shoulder. "Let's think about this. Is Jonas or Rodrigo upset with you about something?"

She shook her head. "No. They've both worked for me before. We've never had any disagreements. Besides, if I leave the island, they're out of jobs."

"It can't be any of my crew," he said. "They didn't even

know you before we arrived here." He glanced at her. "Did they?"

"No. I'd never see any of them before."

"What about Merrick?"

"What about him?"

"Did you know him before?"

"No. I mean, I knew who he was, but we'd never met. Besides, he wasn't even here when I had my first hallucination, or whatever you want to call it."

"He could have been lurking around, but I don't see how he would have gotten on board your boat and slipped you some sort of hallucinogen without your knowing it." He removed his arm from around her and rested his elbows on his knees. "And you've never experienced anything like this before?"

"Never."

"And it only happens when I'm nearby?"

"So far."

"I've had a lot of different effects on women, but I've never caused one to hallucinate before."

He looked so downcast she almost felt sorry for him. She laid her hand on his thigh. "I feel better, knowing you'll try to help me," she said.

"I don't know what I can do."

"I can think of something." She moved his hand to her own thigh, and slid it up to where her leg joined her torso. "You can help me take my mind off whatever's happening."

He turned toward her. "I can do that." He began nibbling her neck, the sensation of his lips against the sensitive flesh of her throat making her stomach flutter wildly.

"I guess Passionata was right," she said.

"How's that?" He transferred his attention to her collarbone.

"The way to a man's heart really is through sex."

"Mmm." He kissed the top of one breast. "Sex is good, but I like you even when we aren't naked."

The flutters increased. This wasn't exactly a declaration of love, but coming from Adam, she considered it high praise. She slid her fingers through his hair and cradled the back of his head. "I like you, too," she said. "Even when you're not naked." Sure, he wasn't the kind of man who was overly concerned with fashion or manners, but he had integrity. He cared about something, even if it was a ship that sank three hundred years ago. He radiated strength and dependability and that was probably the reason why she'd been drawn to him.

"But since we *are* naked…" He encircled her waist and drew her to him, giving her an openmouthed kiss that sent heat clear to her toes.

He laid her back on the chaise, and the desire that had been momentarily cooled by their discussion came roaring back with even greater intensity. Every inch of her was alive to him, so that she trembled at the slightest touch. When his lips closed over her breast, she arched to him, and raked her fingers down his back, reveling in the way his muscles bunched beneath her hands.

When he straddled the lounger and loomed over her, she caught her breath, waiting for the dizziness that had clouded their lovemaking before to return, for the passiveness that had so aggravated her to overtake her once more.

But this time she was fully herself, so before he could enter her, she pushed him away. "I want to be on top," she said.

He grinned. "I remember."

As soon as she stood, he reclined on the chaise, his erection provocatively displayed. "Your ride is ready, m'lady," he said in a truly horrible British accent.

She laughed, her earlier apprehension fleeing. For all the heat and intensity of her encounters with her dream lover, this was what she had missed—the humor and banter of partners who are comfortable with each other and with themselves. How could she ever have believed she had anything to fear from Adam? Sex with him was only about pleasure and fun.

She took her time lowering herself over him, letting him fill her a scant half inch at a time, drawing out the experience, her gaze locked to his, watching his eyes darken, the heat of his stare raising her own temperature.

He grasped her hips, and with her feet planted on either side of the chaise, she experimented with a gentle bounce. He exhaled sharply and she froze, thighs tensed. "Too hard?" she asked.

"No." He squeezed her hips. "No, it felt good." He coaxed her more firmly over him. "Really good."

"Mmm. It feels good from this side, too." She tried again, and soon found a rhythm. At this angle he penetrated her deeply, and she reveled in her ability to control every move. This was how sex should be, both partners giving *and* receiving pleasure.

She massaged her breasts, enjoying knowing that watching her aroused him even more. He reached around to caress her bottom, his hands kneading and stroking, and she was startled by how quickly she felt herself on the edge of climax. She slowed, trying to draw out the sensation, but he arched to meet her, urging a faster pace. She closed her eyes and surrendered to the rush of feelings carrying her farther and higher.

When her climax hit, she felt as if she was soaring, floating, exhilarated and joyous, as if she'd drunk a whole bottle of champagne.

He bucked beneath her, driving himself toward his own climax. As he spent himself in a last few spasms, he reached for her and drew her down to him. They lay together for a long while. He was tender, stroking her hair, kissing her temple. She pressed her cheek to his chest and listened to his heartbeat.

He slid his hand beneath the thin gold chain around her neck and raised his head to examine the gold charm that hung there. "A globe of the world?" he asked.

"My grandmother gave it to me," she said. "She said it represented all the traveling I'd do and the adventures I'd have." She'd been sixteen at the time, a long way from travel and adventures, stuck at home most nights babysitting her younger siblings, wanting desperately to escape the drudgery of her everyday life but not seeing how to go about it. Her grandmother had recognized the restlessness in her, and her gift had acknowledged that anything was possible for a person who was determined. Sandra had worn the globe ever since, a reminder of her grandmother's faith in her and her own ability to achieve any goal she set for herself.

"And have you had adventures?" Adam asked.

"Some." She trailed her hand across his chest. "So have you. I read up on you this past year."

"Oh. What did you find out?"

"That you'd unearthed dinosaur bones in Wyoming and American Indian relics in Utah. I even read a couple of papers you'd written."

He chuckled. "I'm sure you found them thrilling."

"They were a little dry," she admitted. "But very informative. They convinced me you knew what you were doing here on Passionata's Island."

He slid his hand around to cup her breast. "You had doubts?"

"I didn't mean in *bed*." Laughing, she swatted his hand away. "I meant salvaging the *Eve*. You have a talent for finding historical artifacts."

"I don't know if it's a talent so much as hard work."

"Yes, there's that, too." Talent hadn't gotten her where she was today. There were plenty of talented, pretty young women trying to break into the business. Sandra had earned the privilege of putting together her own shows through many long hours of grunt work over the years. A devotion to work was one thing she and Adam had in common.

She closed her eyes, and was almost asleep when he spoke again. "I wonder if there's something on the island that's triggering these attacks or whatever you want to call them that you're having."

"You mean, like an allergic reaction?" Allergies were supposed to cause hives and wheezing, weren't they? She'd never heard of one that gave a person hallucinations— much less multiple orgasms.

"I was thinking more of a psychological reaction."

She raised her head and looked at him. "Are you saying I'm nuts?"

"No. I don't think you're nuts." He gave her arm a comforting squeeze. "But something is messing with your mind, and we know it's not me."

"I'm sorry I ever accused you. But I didn't know what else to think."

"I know. In your position I'd have probably felt the same." He pressed his hand against her back, urging her to lie down again. "Humor me here while I toss out some ideas."

"All right." She settled her head into the hollow of his shoulder once more.

"I wonder if you're identifying with Passionata," he said.

"Identifying?"

"Feeling empathy for her or some kind of strong connection. The two of you aren't so different, you know. Like her, you're a strong woman who's made a name for herself in a profession dominated by men."

She was flattered that he saw this strength in her, but couldn't buy this theory. "That can't be it," she said. "Passionata was powerful and in charge. Whenever these spells come over me I'm so passive I can hardly move. It's one of the things that frustrates me. And who is Frederick? There's no mention of anyone by that name in *Confessions of a Pirate Queen.*"

"Are you sure?"

"Yes. I've read the whole thing twice. Parts of it more than that." After all, some of those scenes were plenty erotic. Inspirational, even.

"And all the times this has happened, there's been some link to Passionata—in the tower where she had her headquarters, and near the wreck of the *Eve,* when I showed you the dagger that came from the ship."

"You're forgetting the very first time—when I had dinner with you. That had nothing to do with Passionata."

"I'd forgotten about that one."

"Yeah." She sighed. "I appreciate your trying to help. Maybe between the two of us, we can eventually figure this out. In the meantime, please don't tell anyone else about this."

"I promise I won't. But I want you to promise me something, too."

"What's that?" She didn't like being obligated to other people, especially a man who already had the ability to keep her emotionally off balance.

"You'll tell me if it happens again. Maybe if I'm there when it's happening, I'll see some clue that will help."

In a way, he already had been there—at least in her fantasies. Or at least she suspected the mysterious Frederick was Adam with another name. Until she saw the dream man's face she couldn't be sure. But she hoped she wouldn't have the opportunity again. Sex with Adam was better—more real and safe—than her dream encounters with the man who had so moved and dominated her. The dream man had taken her to a place where she wasn't herself, while with Adam she was free to be herself—or even better.

He kissed the top of her head and snuggled closer. "I always thought a woman would interfere with my work on a project like this," he said. "But you're starting to make me see things differently. I could get used to this."

He probably only meant that he could get used to regular sex—at least that was her experience with most men, and it was an idea she encouraged. But as much as logic told her the affair with Adam was merely a fun summer fling, deep inside she felt the blossoming of something deeper and more special. She'd already admitted to herself that Adam made her feel things no one else had. But she'd never expected that one of those feelings would be this hope for something more. Some deeper connection or more intense emotional bond.

Something that a less practical, independent woman might even have labeled as love.

9

THE NEXT DAY a bleary-eyed and hungover crew gathered to begin the work of excavating the wreckage site. "The magnetometer does indicate the presence of metal underneath the sand," Adam said when they had gathered around him on the deck of the *Caspian*. Despite his own late night, he was in good spirits—partly due to the prospect of beginning real salvage operations on the wreck, and certainly largely due to his evening's activities with Sandra. Another example of how her presence on the island had contributed to, rather than detracted from, his work.

"We'll use that as a guide as to where to dig and how deep," he continued. "As I said last night, we can't rush in and start tearing things apart. We'll excavate one grid at a time, sifting the sand and documenting everything we find."

"That could take months," Merrick whined.

"We have all summer," Adam said. "So we'd better get busy. We'll work in teams of three. Sam, you work with me and Tessa. Charlie and Brent, you go with Roger."

"What about me?" Merrick asked.

"You can stay up top and help with the equipment," Adam said.

"I'd rather dive."

The earnestness behind the protest made Adam relent.

They could certainly use the help. "Fine," he said. "You can work with Charlie and Brent."

"We'd better keep an eye on the weather," Roger said. "Reports coming in this morning show a tropical depression building off the coast of Africa that could mean trouble."

Adam fought to keep from rolling his eyes over Roger's obsession with the weather. It was important to monitor conditions, but Roger viewed every squall as a potential category-five hurricane bearing down on them. "I don't think we need to worry about a storm that's a thousand miles away," he said.

"You ought to worry," Roger said. "Experts are predicting this will be a bad hurricane season."

"What will you do if there's a hurricane?"

Adam turned and saw Sandra walking toward them. She wore a red-and-yellow sarong knotted over her breasts, her long legs bare. His mind flashed back to her straddling him, naked, her head thrown back as she cried out in passion. He forced his mind away from the image, back to the matter at hand.

"Hello, Sandra." Merrick smiled and hurried to meet her. He took her hand and led her toward their circle. "You're looking lovely as always. I missed you at the party last night. Did you leave early?"

"Yes." She freed her hand from his and brushed back her hair. "I didn't see any need to interrupt everyone's fun to say good-night, so I just slipped away."

"I seem to recall the professor slipped away early also." Charlie grinned at them.

Adam refused to rise to the bait. Everyone could think what they wanted, but he saw no need to flaunt his relationship with Sandra. They were indulging in a private fantasy for the duration of this salvage operation. It wasn't the kind of pairing that would ever stand the test of time or public scrutiny, so why risk it? Better to enjoy each other in secret while they were here on the island, and part at the end of the summer with no regrets. If more people looked at relationships in such a practical way, surely there would be fewer broken hearts and damaged egos to contend with.

"Judging by your bloodshot eyes, I'd say you managed to have a good time without me," Sandra said. She turned to Adam. "What's your backup plan in case of a hurricane?" she asked.

"*If* a hurricane approaches, we'll have plenty of time to prepare," he said. "There's no sense wasting time worrying about it now."

"The weather service says there's a one-in-four chance this area will experience at least one category-three or greater storm this season," Roger said. "If one shows up, we'd better pull anchor and head for someplace out of the storm's path."

"I was reading that a hurricane in 1850 almost wiped Passionata's Island off the map," Charlie said. "That and other storms are one reason it's still uninhabited."

"I'd say the remoteness, lack of a water source other than rain and the fact that the island is infested with birds has more to do with it being uninhabited," Brent said.

"That, and the curse," Tessa said.

Merrick's eyebrows rose. "The curse? What curse?"

"Passionata's curse, of course." Sandra struck a dramatic pose. "As she stood on the gallows, about to be hanged, the infamous pirate queen placed a curse on anyone who disturbed her island sanctuary." She relaxed and shrugged. "Even if there's nothing to it, it makes a great story. And great television. The viewers will love it."

Merrick nodded. "Collectors might, too. A good story can add thousands of dollars to artifacts."

Adam couldn't contain his annoyance over the conversation straying so far afield. "I don't believe in curses, or in worrying about storms that may never get here," he said. "We have to get to work."

"Aye, aye, Captain." Charlie executed a smart salute.

Adam frowned at him. "You all know what to do," he said. "Get busy. I have a couple of things I need to discuss with Sandra before I join you."

Charlie grinned. "Yeah, I'm sure you have important things to discuss." Then he hurried after Tessa and the others.

Adam was left alone on the deck with Sandra—and Merrick. The billionaire ignored Adam's glare, all his attention fixed on Sandra. "Do you need any help with filming today?" he asked.

"No, I have plenty of help," she said. "You don't have to worry about me."

"I certainly don't worry that you're capable," Merrick said, moving closer, until he was practically touching her. "I've always had an interest in documentary filming. In fact, I've often thought of funding a documentary or short film. You'd be the perfect person to help me with the project."

A frown flashed across her forehead, but she quickly resumed a look of cool indifference. "My schedule is really crowded for the foreseeable future," she said. "You probably should find someone else to help you. I can give you some names."

"I'm willing to wait," Merrick said. "I really only want a top-rate professional like you. Maybe the two of us could get together and discuss this later."

Maybe so many women fell over themselves chasing after his billions that Merrick had never bothered to perfect his flirting skills, Adam thought. As limited as his own experience was, even he knew any woman worth knowing would see through such blatant flattery.

Sandra didn't waste her time replying to Merrick's offer. She turned to Adam. "What did you need to talk to me about?" she asked. Though her voice and face remained calm, Adam didn't miss the momentary flare of heat in her eyes, and he felt a corresponding warmth within himself as once more memories of last night flooded his consciousness.

He leaned closer to her, trying to shut Merrick out of their circle altogether. "I don't think there'll be much good footage today," he said.

"Let me send Jonas and Albert down for a few establishing shots," she said. "Then we can begin taping interviews with some of the crew members."

"You could interview me," Merrick said, inserting himself between them once more.

"And why would my viewers be interested in you?" Sandra asked.

"I know a lot about the shipwreck and the treasure that's supposed to be down there. Besides, I want to hear more about this curse."

"I need to speak with the crew about their roles in the search first," Sandra said. The smile she gave Merrick was so warm Adam saw red. He sucked in a deep breath to clear his head and steady himself.

He reminded himself Sandra didn't need him to defend her. She was doing a good job of that on her own.

"Mr. Merrick?" Tessa hurried toward them once more, and stopped before them, slightly out of breath. "I'm sorry to interrupt, but Roger wants to speak with you," she said.

"He wants to speak to me?" Merrick glanced at Sandra, then directed his attention to Tessa once more. "What about?"

"I don't know, he just asked me to fetch you." She touched his arm. "Come on, I'll take you to him."

Merrick looked confused. "All right. If it's that urgent." He turned to Sandra. "I hope we can talk later. I'm sure I have things to say that your viewers would find interesting. And I'm sure you and I could find all kinds of topics to discuss."

As he and Tessa walked away, Tessa glanced over her shoulder at Sandra and winked, then ducked her head and hurried after Merrick.

"What was that about?" Adam asked.

"I think Tessa was doing me a favor. She knew I didn't really want to hang out with Merrick."

Adam studied his intern's retreating figure. "Does she know something's going on between you and me?"

Sandra moved closer. "I think any normally perceptive woman who saw us together would suspect something." She leaned toward him, the side of her breast brushing his arm.

"Oh?" He had trouble squeezing that single syllable out past the sudden constriction of his vocal chords. He cleared his throat and tried again. "Why is that?"

"Oh, subtle signals we females pick up on," she said, her gaze locked to his, her lips slightly parted in a way that made him think of long, drugging kisses.

"What kind of signals?"

"The way my eyes dilate when I look at you." She trailed the first two fingers of one hand down his arm. "A softening of my voice when we speak."

She caught his ring finger between her thumb and index finger and began stroking up and down, the suggestiveness of the gesture burning into his brain. He cleared his throat again. "Maybe she noticed your erect nipples pressed against that thin sarong," he said. "I know I did, and I bet Merrick did, too."

She smiled. "Maybe I'm cold." She dropped her hand to the fly of his trunks. "Or maybe she noticed how tight your swim trunks are all of a sudden."

The moment she touched him, all Adam could think of was getting her alone again. Forget the treasure or the film or Merrick or anything but being naked with her again. He'd never known anything like the intensity of the heat between them, as if his libido had lain dormant all these years, waiting for her to show up and awaken it. Now that she was here, every encounter was heavy with the sense of making up for lost time.

Or maybe it was only that he was more aware of his mortality as he approached his fortieth birthday, and his body was sending signals that he was past the age when most men married and reproduced.

It was only Sandra's luck—good or bad, depending on her point of view—that made her the target of this evolutionary urgency.

She leaned forward and planted a soft kiss on his cheek. A silken lock of hair brushed his jaw and he caught the faint scent of tropical flowers from her skin. "We'd both better get to work now," she said. "But later on, let's ditch everyone else and meet at my yacht again. I have a few things I want to show you."

He blinked, but before he could find his voice to ask, "what things?" she was walking away, the sway of her hips mesmerizing him, like the pendulum of a clock, ticking away the seconds until they'd be together again.

ONE OF THE BLESSINGS—and the banes—of working on a remote island was the lack of communication with the outside world via telephone, cell phone or e-mail. A satellite phone was available for summoning help in case of an emergency, and the occasional yachter who anchored off the island could be persuaded to pass along letters, but other than that the workers of this project were cut off from the rest of civilization.

So Sandra was startled when one morning a few days later Rodrigo knocked on her cabin door as she was getting ready for the day. "A call's come in for you," he said.

"A call?" She wondered if she'd heard him correctly. "Who is it?"

Rodrigo shook his head. "He didn't say. Only that he needed to speak with you."

Heart pounding, she pushed past Rodrigo and raced toward the navigation room where the satellite phone was kept. Had something happened to her grandmother? Was one of her brothers or sisters hurt?

"Hello? This is Sandra Newman." She held a headset with one hand and clamped the other on to the back of a chair, trying to steady herself.

"Sandra! Why haven't I heard anything out of you? Where's all this fabulous footage of pirate treasure you promised me?"

Her fingers tightened around the chair back and she recognized the voice of her producer, Gary Simon. "I can't believe you wasted your time and mine calling me like this," she said. "You'll see the film when it's done."

"No, I want to see some preliminaries," Gary said. "I took a risk funding this wild idea of yours, and I need to prove that I made the right decision."

"You'll see the film when it's done," she repeated, deliberately keeping her voice coolly professional.

"I have bosses to answer to, you know," Gary said. "I need to prove to them I didn't make a mistake giving you another chance."

"Your faith in me is touching," she said. "I'm the one who took the real risk here. I'm putting my reputation on the line."

"Your reputation right now is as a former star who no longer has what it takes to pull in the ratings," Gary snapped. "I'm putting the studio's money and my job on the line for you, so don't talk to me about risk."

White-hot anger blurred her vision, and it took everything in her not to hurl the phone across the room. Gary's criticism stung, as he'd meant it to; the sliver of truth behind it hurt even worse. At thirty-six she was dangerously close to being a has-been in the glamorous world of television. She hoped this documentary would solidify her reputation as a talent both behind and in front of the camera, and extend her career accordingly.

"What have you got so far?" Gary asked.

"I've got some great footage of the island and some establishing shots of the wreck. And I've started interviewing some of the crew members about their role in the search."

"But no treasure?" Gary muttered a curse. "I knew it. So help me, Sandra, if you don't come up with gold and silver and jewels—the kind of loot people think of as real pirate's treasure, both our asses are in a sling."

"Get a grip," she said. For a man in charge of a major network, Gary could be a huge whiner. "Adam's barely started the recovery work, though he's already found some interesting artifacts." Though she doubted Gary would think a rusty dagger and a few gold coins were enough to wow viewers.

"Who the hell is Adam?"

"Professor Carroway. He's in charge of the salvage operation. He's uncovered some interesting artifacts—"

"A bunch of rusty spoons won't cut it," Gary said. "The

network is losing ground to shows like *Celebrity Dance Off* and *Real-Life Prince Charming*. Shows that are a hell of a lot cheaper to produce than a hunt for make-believe treasure in some godforsaken corner of the globe."

"The treasure is not make-believe," Sandra said.

"For both our sakes, I hope not."

"Don't panic until you've seen the final film. I have to get to work now. Goodbye." She hung up and exhaled a long breath, then carefully lowered herself into the chair she'd been holding on to. She'd told Gary not to panic, but she needed to follow her own advice. What if she was wasting the studio's money—and her reputation—on an expensive chase after the equivalent of a few rusty spoons? She'd be back to reporting on city council meetings for some third-market station in Oklahoma—and her family would chide her for thinking herself better than she should be. Her mother and sisters had never understood why, if remaining in their small town working menial jobs and raising babies was good enough for them, it wasn't good enough for Sandra, as well.

"Excuse me, Sandra?"

She looked up to find Rodrigo standing in the doorway. "What is it?" she asked.

"While you were on the telephone, one of Mr. Merrick's men delivered this." He handed her a folded sheet of white linen stationery.

Frowning, she unfolded the note.

The pleasure of your company is requested aboard the Lucy this evening at 7:30 p.m. for dinner.

I'm looking forward to seeing you, Damian.

The last line was scrawled beneath the typewritten invitation. She refolded the note and returned it to Rodrigo. "Send my regrets." It was the third such invitation this week, all of which she'd declined, but Merrick kept trying. Was he convinced he could wear her down, or so obtuse he wasn't getting the message?

She was too preoccupied for a social dinner this evening, anyway. Gary's phone call had upset her more than she wanted anyone to know. What if Adam and his crew cleared the wreck site and found nothing more than rusty metal and barnacles? Adam might be satisfied with a handful of artifacts, but Gary wouldn't be.

Which meant she and Adam would end up in the same boat—so to speak—unlikely to secure funding for their next projects, their professional reputations in tatters. Some people might say they could at least seek solace in each other's arms, but frankly she didn't see either of them finding any comfort in failure. If anything, a mutual defeat would be likely to drive them apart.

So if she wanted to keep her job, her reputation and Adam, she had better hope for something besides old barrel hoops under the litter scattered across the ocean floor.

Speaking of keeping, since when had she started thinking about "keeping" Adam? Apparently, since now. The idea started a warm glow deep in the center of her chest. The man was stubborn, independent, arrogant and infuriating—in other words, he was a lot like Sandra herself, something she'd failed to notice before this instant. Maybe that explained her deep, persistent attraction to him. On the surface they were from different worlds, all wrong for each other. But maybe sometimes, like now, two wrongs really did make a right.

10

"THE LATEST REPORTS show Tropical Storm Darryl headed this way," Roger announced when he joined the others on the beach Friday. The crew gathered here every afternoon to discuss the day's progress and deal with any problems that had cropped up.

Tired and frustrated from yet another day spent sifting through almost worthless debris at the wreck site, the weather was one problem Adam didn't want to hear about. But it had to be addressed. "A tropical storm shouldn't endanger us," he said. "We can easily ride out a storm that size. We'll need to make sure all our equipment is secured and wait it out." With any luck they'd only need to miss a day of diving, a day that could be spent organizing and cataloging their finds so far.

"What if it turns into a hurricane?" Roger asked. "You're not going to try to ride that out, are you?"

The man's pessimism, disguised as common sense, grated on Adam's nerves. "It's not a hurricane yet, is it?" he said. "Keep watching the weather reports. Tell me when we have something to really worry about. Until then, don't bother me."

"Bother you about what?" Damian strode across the beach toward them. Fresh from the shower, his hair was slicked back, a towel slung around his shoulders. He looked as if he'd just emerged from the country-club pool. "Do you think we'll locate the treasure soon?" he asked, stopping in front of Adam. "We've spent all this time photographing, measuring, drawing, cleaning and storing bits of wood and scraps of iron. When do we get to the gold?"

"Those bits of wood and scraps of iron could be as historically significant as gold," Adam said. "We'll spend another month—or more—if that's what it takes to collect and catalog everything at the site."

Merrick looked petulant. "When are we going to locate the treasure we came here to find?" he demanded.

"We'll find it." Adam turned away, annoyed at having to continually justify his actions to this man whose only claim of authority was having had the luck to be born with a bunch of money to hold over Adam's head. Merrick hadn't spent years studying Passionata and her island, using his vacation time and own scant funds to search for her ship. He might have money invested in this project, but Adam had invested *himself*.

"What if we don't find it?" Merrick's voice was more strident than usual.

"We'll find it." Adam turned to face the billionaire once more.

Merrick crossed his arms over his chest and glanced at the others as if to make sure he had an audience. "I'm beginning to wonder if this wreck really is the *Eve*," he said. "Maybe it's some hapless freighter that happened to sink here with no more valuable cargo than barrel staves and ballast."

Adam didn't miss the looks exchanged between Roger and Sam, and between Tessa and Brent, looks that confirmed their own doubts. Adam's stomach churned. "It has to be the *Eve*," he said. "It's in the exact location my research indicates." But he had been teaching long enough to know research wasn't always accurate. His own belief in the wreck meant no more than wishes on the moon. The others knew these things, also. "I don't have time to debate this with you," he said. "There's a storm coming in and we have to get ready."

"I'm ready to continue my interviews," Sandra said. She'd constructed a makeshift set down the beach, where she spent part of every afternoon interviewing various members of the salvage team about their reasons for joining the expedition and their experiences so far, though Adam doubted the attention of many male viewers would be focused on the divers. They'd all be watching Sandra who, dressed in a hot orange string bikini and gold belly chain, with an orange hibiscus blossom tucked behind one ear, could probably drive up her ratings by simply standing still in front of the camera.

"If the weather's taking a turn for the worse, I'd better hurry to finish them up," she said, but made no move to stir from Adam's side.

Having her there made him feel calmer. She was the one person who didn't rub him the wrong way at the moment. It could be said she knew how to rub him exactly the right way, as evidenced by how much time they'd spent together in the evenings, employing elaborate strategies in order to sneak away from the others and be alone.

Last night, for instance, he'd announced he was going night fishing, and as soon as he was out of sight of shore he'd swung the dinghy around and rowed to Sandra's yacht, where she'd greeted him at the door of her cabin wearing only a smile and red high heels.

He'd forgotten all about the fishing ruse until Charlie asked him at breakfast if he'd caught anything.

"I must have been using the wrong kind of bait," he'd mumbled around a mouthful of toast.

"I don't think we really have anything to worry about from this storm," he said. He smiled, but she didn't return the look. In fact, she seemed preoccupied.

"Maybe not." Roger spat on the sand. "But I think we should prepare for the worst and hope it doesn't come to that. If it does, at least we'll be ready."

"What do we need to do to get ready?" Tessa asked.

While the others fell into a debate about what should be done, Adam pulled Sandra aside and walked with her a short distance down the beach. "Is something wrong?" he asked.

"I had another call from my producer," she said. "On the satellite phone I keep for emergencies."

"*Another* call? Is everything all right back home?" Did she have family? Parents, siblings—even a child? For all the intimacy they'd shared, he realized he didn't know much about her life away from the island.

"He called once before." She made a face. "Same song, second verse. He's worried about his investment. He wanted to know if I had any footage of gold and jewels yet. Something to prove to him he hadn't wasted the network's money."

So Merrick wasn't the only one making a fuss about their slow progress. "What did you tell him?"

"I told him the film isn't finished yet. That he needs to wait."

"What did he say?"

Her eyes met his at last, her expression intense. "He said a few rusty spoons wasn't going to be enough. That the network is losing money to reality-TV shows on other stations, which are cheap to produce and very popular. If this documentary doesn't make a big splash, he and I could both be out of jobs."

"Yeah. People won't exactly be lining up to shake my hand or take my classes, either."

She folded her arms across her chest. "Do you think we're close?" she asked. "Is there more than the few gold coins and the dagger underneath all this junk you've been pulling out all week?"

"If it's anywhere, it's there," he said, his earlier confidence sliding with each assault by doubters. "We'll know for sure in a day or two."

She nodded. "I'm really glad Gary is two thousand miles away."

"Yeah." Adam only wished Merrick was stuck back in the States. Or Iceland. Or hell. Anywhere a long way away from Passionata's Island.

"Brent is ready for his interview," Jonas called from the makeshift set, where he'd set up his camera facing out toward the ocean.

"I'd better go," Sandra said, and hurried away.

He watched her greet Brent with a smile. She'd already interviewed most of the others, though she'd made no mention of talking on camera with Adam. Maybe she was saving the best for the last.

Or maybe she was waiting for more proof that all this was worth the effort before she committed to capturing him on film.

As soon as he found treasure and proved it was from the *Eve,* he'd be a hero.

But if he found nothing, he'd be a laughingstock. There was no middle ground in this business.

Merrick broke away from the others and headed toward Adam. Unwilling to be drawn into another debate, Adam turned and headed toward his own yacht. If Merrick had the nerve to follow, Adam would pull up the ladder and refuse to let him board.

But Merrick didn't follow. Adam retrieved a beer from

the galley and stretched out in a lounge chair on deck—
the same chair where he and Sandra had had such energetic
and satisfying sex less than two weeks ago. He sipped the
beer and smiled, remembering. His uncle Benny would
have liked Sandra. He always said a woman who had a
sense of adventure was worth knowing.

Knowing but not marrying. Benny had no use for anything or anyone that might keep him tied down. He was the
black sheep of the family, the only one of his brothers and
sisters who had turned his back on a conventional life of
steady job and family for the unpredictable lot of part-
time dockworker and full-time sailor. The *Double Dare* had
been his home for all the years Adam had known him, and
the two of them had spent many happy hours on this very
deck, out of reach of the disapproving stares and stern
lectures of Benny's sister, Faye, who was Adam's mother.

"My boy is smart, and he's going to make something of
himself," Faye had told Benny. "He's going to be a doctor
or a lawyer, or own his own business. So don't go filling
his head full of a lot of nonsense and your sea stories."

But Adam had begged his uncle to repeat over and over
the tales of his own experience, and the historical sea lore
he'd collected over the years. While his parents pushed him
to study hard, learn social graces and make a name for himself, he'd preferred to spend his free time sailing, listening
to Benny and daydreaming about traveling to the past.

When Adam had announced he intended to major in
history and devote himself to teaching and research, his
mother hadn't spoken to him for six months. Even now her
communications were tinged with disappointment. Ironi-
cally, Adam realized his appearance in Sandra's documentary would validate him more for his parents than all the
scholarly publications or academic acclaim he'd managed

to accumulate over the years. Fame and wealth were the two things that would allow his mother and father to brag to their friends about their only son, though Adam cared little for either.

What he wanted was the validation of the hard work he'd put in over the years, and the realization of his boyhood dream to travel to the past. As he sat on his boat, drinking the beer, he could almost hear Uncle Benny cheering him on. "Following your own course isn't easy," Benny had said. "But when you get to where you want to go, it's the best high in the world. And you'll know you did it all by yourself."

As a boy, those words had thrilled Adam, but now the other meaning of this declaration of independence gave him pause. Finding the *Eve* was a wonderful victory, but less sweet because he had no one to share the feeling. When all was said and done, self-reliance could be a lonely business. And the older he was, the more the loneliness bothered him.

But he wasn't sure what to do about it. He'd never found it easy to let down his guard with women. Maybe they sensed this. All his relationships so far had required little from either side. They offered companionship, sex and a social outlet from his academic work. Often they were women who needed him for one reason or another. Some might say he let women use him, but the truth was he liked being depended on.

But none of those women had the sense of adventure Uncle Benny had so praised. It had been easier to find his adventure elsewhere, hunting treasures from the past. Every summer for several years he'd participated in expeditions headed by others—volunteering with an archeological crew in Mexico, hunting for mastodon bones in the Black

Hills and restoring Native American middens in Utah—but this was his first solo project, the dream that had captivated him from the moment he'd heard of Passionata's Island.

Leaving his empty beer bottle on the deck, he shoved out of the chaise and headed for his cabin. He had to prove that this wreck was the *Eve.* He sat at the fold-down desk and sifted through the research material piled there. What would provide the clue he needed to make a breakthrough?

He set aside charts, notebooks and aerial photos of the island, and picked up a copy of *Confessions of a Pirate Queen.* Much of the book was believed to be apocryphal, but there was definitely some truth in it. He flipped through the small volume, looking for a description of the ship, something about the size or style, the configuration of the mast, typical cargo and crew, munitions—anything he could match with what they'd found so far at the wreck site.

In Tortuga, I rechristened my father's ship the *Eve.* She was a galley, low and fast, able to outrun all pursuers. I chose the name Eve after that first woman, who had eaten the forbidden fruit of knowledge, and had her eyes opened to the truth. As my eyes had been opened to the truth about men, and one man in particular. I gave myself to him body and soul, but he was not content with only these things. He took from me my very life, laying waste to all he had claimed to love.

A curse upon him! I have no need of him. No need of my old self. I leave Jane Hallowell behind, a martyr to a young girl's foolishness. Yet I mourn her passing, sorrowful in both spirit and body.

Though hatred for my betrayer burns in my soul, desire for him still flames in my body. He taught me all the joys of intimate congress. I was passion's apt pupil, discovering a pleasure more potent than that of those who frequent the opium parlors, yet every bit as addictive.

The man I had loved had stabbed me and caused a wound that, while not mortal, has scarred me forever. In those long hours when I could not sleep, I made a vow to never speak his name again. And I would not quietly kill myself as others thought proper, but I would venture into the world, to places where no proper woman dared show her face. I would walk proudly and I would never again allow a man to get the best of me. I would wreak my revenge upon them all, and show them who is truly the weaker sex.

I would take them as my lovers and use them as my betrayer had used me. But I would never trust them. I would never trust anyone, but especially no man.

Adam closed the book. So much for any description of the *Eve*. He'd been grasping at straws thinking he'd learn anything about the ship from Passionata's book, though he'd learned more about the pirate queen herself. He could relate to her reluctance to trust anyone. He'd spent his life looking upon other people—especially women—with skepticism. Now that he was almost forty, he didn't know if he could change that.

Or even if he should.

ALONE IN HER CABIN after supper, Sandra reviewed the tape of her interview with Brent. With a spiral-bound notebook opened on the desk beside her, she made note of some good quotes, and jotted down ideas about where this clip might fit in the production that was shaping up. Back in the States she'd edit everything together, do the voice-over and cut in some staged retellings of Passionata's history. This was good stuff. The kind of thing that could reignite her career.

If they found treasure. She needed stacks of silver ingots, piles of gold coins, chests of jewels. That was the kind of thing that took people's breath away.

But how did she know the *Eve* even carried the kind of things she was looking for? Yes, it was a pirate ship, but maybe Passionata only used it as her flagship and had other ships do the work of gathering up the booty from her raids. Sandra opened her desk and rifled through the drawers until she came to her copy of *Confessions of a Pirate Queen.* The paperback volume was worn from her frequent readings, but she couldn't remember if there were any references in there to the kind of things Passionata and her crew robbed from other ships.

Sandra sat on the edge of her bed and flipped through the book, then began to read.

The capture of the *Saint Claire* was our most prosperous raid to date, and we returned to the island to celebrate and divide the spoils. But the most interesting booty to me was a man—a sailor with skin the color of cocoa beans and eyes that burned through me as he stood before me. His hands and feet were shackled, but he held his head high.

"What is your name?" I asked him.

"Roman," he replied, his gaze locked to mine.

"Do you know who I am, Roman?"

"I have heard you called the pirate queen."

I smiled at this. The title pleased me, though it was not one I had sought. I put a hand on his shoulder, which was hard with muscle, his skin warmed from the intense sun. "Do you know the fate of the men I capture?" I asked him.

Still his gaze did not waver. "Some say you make them your slaves. Others, your lovers."

"And which would you prefer?"

"I am no man's—or woman's—slave."

Did I imagine the sudden flare of heat in his eyes? I ordered the guard to unchain him, then took his hand in mine. "Come with me," I said. "We'll see if you are worthy to share my bed."

When we were alone in my chambers at the top of the tower, I ordered him to remove his clothes. He balked. "I am not used to taking orders from a woman," he said.

"And I am not used to having my orders questioned. Perhaps you prefer to be a slave after all." I turned my back and made as if to summon a guard.

"I have never had a relationship where I was not in charge," Roman said, his voice calm, presenting a fact, not an argument.

And I had not been subject to any man's wishes since the one who betrayed me had last undressed me and claimed me for his own, even as he was plotting against me. I turned to face him once more. "No woman is free to experience full enjoyment of passion as long as she is not also free to command her own life," I told him.

"The same could be said of any man."

"But men have been free since the day of creation. It is time they were made to see life from another perspective—and to learn what women will teach them."

The corner of his mouth twitched, as if he was amused. "And what will you teach me?"

"That true delight is to be found in giving a woman free rein." I gestured to him again. "Now take off those clothes."

He didn't hesitate this time. I felt my nipples tighten as he removed his shirt, my thighs moisten as he stepped out of his trousers, revealing a thick, erect member, his balls hanging heavy amidst a thatch of dark, wiry hair.

He stood tall, legs apart, hands on his hips, proudly displaying himself. What is it in men that gives them this pride, while we women rush to hide our nakedness, as if there is something shameful in breasts and belly? Even I, as practiced as I was, had to fight a secret sliver of shame as I undid the buttons of my gown.

But I stood before him as proudly as any man ever posed for me, and I saw the approval in his eyes as he walked toward me.

I put out a hand to forestall him. "Remember, I am in charge," I said. "I say when you will touch me."

His expression clouded, but he said nothing, merely stopped and waited.

I walked around him, admiring the straight line of his back, the tight curve of his buttocks. I trailed my fingers across the cool, smooth flesh of his backside and felt him shiver at my touch, all the while the heat within me building to a fever pitch. I wanted this man, and I needed him to ease the ache inside me—

A knock on the door jolted Sandra from her reading. She looked up and it came again. She shoved the book under her pillow and went to answer it.

Adam stood in the hallway, his broad shoulders filling the narrow space. She stared at him, still lost in the eighteenth century. Reading Passionata's words, Sandra had become the pirate queen. She had been the one seducing the sexy sailor. The fantasy had been so realistic her breasts ached, and she felt the hot dampness of arousal between her thighs.

"Are you all right?" Adam asked, frowning at her.

"No," she said. "Not exactly."

"What's wrong? Did you have another of your spells?"

"No, it isn't that."

"Then what is it?"

She grabbed the front of his shirt and dragged him into her cabin and kicked the door shut behind her. "I need you," she said. "Now." Before he could answer she wrapped herself around him, pulled his head down to hers and kissed him long and hard, plunging her tongue into his mouth the way she wanted him to plunge his cock into her. Later they could talk. Right now she needed a night of hot, hard sex, and he was just the man to give it to her.

11

SANDRA'S ENTHUSIASTIC greeting caught Adam off guard, but he quickly got into the spirit of the moment. She was a woman on fire, her body shaped to his, her mouth seeking, her hands tearing at his clothes. Within seconds they were both naked. She nipped at his shoulder and wrapped one leg around him, the wet heat of her arousal making his erection tighten painfully.

"I don't know what's gotten into you, but I like it," he said, caressing her buttocks, then moving his hands up and around to cradle her breasts. Her nipples beaded at his touch, and he stroked them with his thumbs as she arched against him.

He was about to bend down and kiss her breast when she leaned forward and took his nipple into her mouth, tugging the nub between her teeth, sending a shock wave straight to his cock. He jerked against her and he felt her lips curve in a smile. "Do you like that?" she asked. "Does that make you hot?"

"You make me hot."

She raised her head and shoved him against the wall, her fingers digging into the muscles of his arms, the heat in her eyes nearly scorching him. Then she wrapped her hand around his erection and began to stroke, up, down and around, until his vision fogged and he knew he was in danger of losing it all.

He pushed her away and tried to catch his breath. "Slow down," he said.

"No. I'm not in the mood to slow down." She grabbed him by the wrist and wrapped her arms around him. "I want you in me. Now. Right here."

Her urgency was contagious, driving him to boost her onto his thighs as he slid into her. She was slick with her arousal and he sank deeply with his first thrust. She clenched around him, stealing his breath, and began to rock against him.

It was intense, physical sex, obliterating thought, stealing the ability to speak, focusing every movement and sense on the need building inside of them. He came hard, unable to hold back, but continued to move in her until he felt her shudder with her own climax.

She rested her forehead against his shoulder, breathing heavily. Holding her tightly, he staggered to the bed, where they collapsed, still in each other's arms. "Feeling better?" he muttered into her shoulder.

"Oh, yeah," she breathed. "You?"

"Yeah. I'm good."

It had been a surprising, amazing encounter, but it had also had a desperate quality, as if Sandra was trying to blot out a bad memory or shake off an obsession. He rolled out of her arms and shoved himself farther up the bed, until his head was resting on a pillow. She crawled up beside him and lay facing him.

He brushed her hair off her shoulder. "Want to tell me what brought this on?" he asked. "Not that I'm complaining," he added. "I might want to duplicate the experience sometime."

Her cheeks flushed pink. "I was reading *Confessions of a Pirate Queen* and I guess I got carried away."

He laughed. "That woman was obsessed with sex."

"She was, but it's more than that." She settled into her pillow. "I think she spent her whole life trying to get back at the man who broke her heart."

"The pirate who betrayed her?"

"Yeah." She looked thoughtful. "It's funny, but even after all those years, I think Passionata died loving him. She could never get over that."

"I can't imagine feeling that way about anyone—especially someone who'd essentially taken everything from me and led to my father's suicide."

"It's a testament to the power of love," she said.

"Or of obsession."

They fell silent after that, and he was almost asleep when her voice pulled him from the edge of slumber. "What brings you to my cabin this evening?" she asked. "Or did you just want sex?"

"I always want sex with you, but I'd have probably made a little small talk first."

"You're such a gentleman."

Why had he stopped by this evening? Oh, yeah. "I wanted to ask if I could review the film you've made so far."

She stiffened. "Why? Are you worried I've portrayed you in an unflattering light?"

"Nothing like that," he assured her. "I want to see if I can spot anything I've missed. Something that might point to the location of more valuable artifacts."

"Treasure."

He nodded.

"You're welcome to look at the film," she said. "I'll have Jonas make a copy and drop it off at your yacht tomorrow." She touched his wrist. "What will you do if the treasure isn't there?"

The knot returned to the pit of his stomach. "I don't

know," he confessed. "I've been so certain, but I'm really only playing a hunch. My colleagues would laugh me out of the room if they knew. I can't explain it, but I've been certain ever since I laid eyes on the wreck."

She raised up on one elbow to face him. "Want to know something funny? I'm sure, too." She smiled. "Call it women's intuition. You're going to find your treasure."

Her confidence in him made him feel as if he could do anything. "I'm glad I found you," he said.

Her smile faded and she looked uncomfortable. He cursed the impulsive words. She'd made it clear from day one that she saw him as an amusing fling. She wasn't interested in a serious relationship any more than he was. He lay on his back and stared at the ceiling, letting the moment pass.

"I'm counting on you to find that treasure," she said after a moment, and eased onto her own back. "I really don't want any more complaining calls from my producer."

"I can't believe he called you on the SAT phone. Twice."

"Me, neither. My first thought was that something had happened to my parents or brothers and sister."

"How many brothers and sisters do you have?"

"Two brothers and a sister. All younger. What about you?"

"I'm an only kid. My parents are retired and live in Arizona."

"I dated a guy once who owned a string of condominiums in Arizona."

"You ever been married?" he asked.

She hesitated. It wasn't an unreasonable question. But had only idle curiosity prompted it, or something more? "I've never been married," she said. "Too involved in my career, I guess. What about you?"

"Nope. Never thought about it much, really. I don't think women see me as husband material."

She faced him once more. "Come on. You've got a good job, you're good-looking and you're not a jerk. That's all most women need."

"You make me sound so exciting."

"You can be pretty exciting." She trailed one finger along his arm. "Lying here with you now is making me excited."

"Oh, yeah?" He rolled toward her.

"Yeah." Desire was building inside her again, like the tide slowly filling a pool, warming her skin and making her heart beat faster. Her earlier urgency had been replaced by this pleasant gradual climb. She cuddled up to Adam and gave him a long, slow kiss, parting her lips and running the tip of her tongue across his teeth, delighting in the sizzle of awareness that spread through her.

His hand on one hip, he drew her close, letting her feel his erection pressed against her stomach. Her smile broadened. Nothing like a man who could keep up with her in bed. There was no denying the incredible chemistry between them, no matter the cause.

They took their time, letting the heat build, exploring one another's bodies, using fingers, lips and tongues to trace the curves and valleys of shoulder and waist, chest and thigh. She nibbled at his shoulder, laughing when he flinched in surprise, pretending to fight him off as he rolled her onto her back and loomed over her. "So you want to play rough, do you?" he asked. "I'll show you." He bent and blew a raspberry on her stomach, and laughter bubbled out of her. She couldn't remember the last time she'd felt this playful with a man, this at ease. It added a wonderful spice to the sex, a different warmth than the intense heat that had marked their earlier encounter.

Then her laughter turned to a sigh as he slid farther down her body, feathering kisses over her abdomen, down over the thatch of curls between her legs, where he gently parted her folds and licked her. She felt the contact all the way up through her body, a shock wave of desire burning through her.

One hand resting on her stomach, as if to steady her, he continued to lick and fondle with the kind of attention to detail she'd seen him give the uncovering of a pewter cup or length of chain from the ocean floor. There was something to be said for getting involved with the analytical type, she thought as she sank farther down in the bed toward him. They were always studying, looking for ways to improve their performance. Not that she'd had any complaints before now, but Adam had obviously done his homework.

And then such thoughts drifted away as she lost herself in the blissed-out sensations his attentions produced. Whereas before she'd felt frantic, fighting her way toward her release, now she basked in the warmth of a slow expansion, the tension and pressure within her climbing steadily upward toward a summit she was confident would be no less incredible for its subtle growth.

Adam shifted his weight and slid one hand up to fondle her breast, and gently tweaked her nipple. That one touch and she went off like a rocket, her climax blossoming within her, filling her with the sensation of light and heat and a bubbly joy.

She didn't even realize she was smiling until he lowered himself over her and looked down into her face. "Did I do that?" he asked.

"Do what?"

"Put that grin on your face."

She tried to look stern, but it was no use. The grin was wider than ever. "I think you did," she said, and pulled him down toward her. "I bet I can make you smile like this, too."

"That's a bet I'd be happy to lose." Then he entered her, sliding slowly, filling her inch by inch. She spread her legs wide, wrapping them around him, urging him deeper, her entreaties turning to soft moans as he began to move within her.

Each stroke was steady and complete, almost but not quite leaving her, then sinking into her again, the delicious friction stoking the fires within her once more. He reached down and fondled her clit and she looked up at him, her vision blurring. "Oh, Adam," she cried as another climax rocked her.

"Nice to hear you say my name," he said, and picked up the pace of his movements, thrusting harder and faster, his body tensed, expression focused inward, until he, too, found his release.

They lay in each other's arms, fully sated, too weary or unwilling to move. After a while she heard his breathing slow and deepen, and she knew he was asleep. She lay awake, pondering all that happened this evening.

When she'd answered the door, she'd been possessed by lust, her physical need for him overruling any restraint or subtlety. That encounter had been remarkable for its rawness and power, its physical intensity and animal passion.

Their second coupling had been no less intense, but different, and not only because their movements had been slower and more deliberate. Earlier in the evening, Adam had been a man to whom she was powerfully attracted, one who was willing and even eager to have sex with her, whose appetites matched her own, someone who filled a need.

But later, when she'd lain in his arms and traced the curve of his biceps and the narrow ridge that marked the scar on his thigh, when she'd pressed her body to his and felt him harden at her touch, when she'd looked into his eyes and seen his desire only for her, it was as if this particular man—Professor Adam Carroway—had become as real and precious to her as her own body.

Before, she'd been having sex with a desirable man. The second time she'd been making love to Adam, a man like no other she'd ever known.

Being with him felt so comfortable. So right. She never felt that way with men. So much of her relationships with the opposite sex had been antagonistic—competitive, each person out to prove something. Adam was the first man in a long time, maybe ever, who she didn't feel the need to impress. He wasn't the type to be impressed. and when he looked at her. she felt as if he already knew everything about her.

Which was crazy. As crazy as her believing the wreck was the *Eve* with no real evidence beyond Adam's say-so. She wasn't the type of person who relied on intuition or gut feelings, but there she had it. Something told her this wreck was a big, important deal. The same something that told her she was safe with Adam.

It was an odd sensation, and one she didn't want to get too comfortable with. The only way to succeed in her business was to keep her edge. She didn't want anyone—even a sexy guy like Adam—tempting her to get dull and complacent. She was Sandra Newman, hard-hitting investigative journalist and documentary filmmaker. In her personal life she was Sandra the temptress or Sandra the ball breaker. There was no room in either of those lives for warm and fuzzy. No room for getting comfortable and letting go, the way Adam tempted her to do.

ADAM WOKE DISORIENTED, unsure of where he was or what had disturbed his slumber. Then he felt Sandra curled beside him and remembered he was in her cabin on her yacht. As he came more awake, he realized the ship was rocking on rough seas, rain pounding at the porthole like gravel tossed against a window, wind whistling across the bow.

He was pulling on his shorts when Sandra spoke to him out of the darkness. "Is that a storm I hear?" she asked.

"Probably that tropical storm Roger was talking about."

She sat up, the sheet gathered around her, and switched on the lamp beside the bed. "Where are you going?"

"I need to make sure my yacht is secure, then check on the equipment on the *Caspian*." He pulled his shirt over his head.

"You can't go out in this," she said. She glanced toward the porthole. "It's pitch-dark out there. Besides, the crew will take care of everything on the *Caspian*."

"I'll be all right. I'll borrow rain gear from one of your crew."

"Adam, no. There's nothing you can do. Stay here with me."

"And do what?"

She smiled. "I can think of a few things." She let the sheet drop from her shoulders, her naked breasts pink and gold in the soft lamplight. Her hair fell in tousled waves around her shoulders, and her eyes looked sleepy and seductive.

He turned away, searching for his deck shoes. "I won't say I'm not tempted," he said. "But I can't stay here letting other people look after my project."

She sighed. "Of course you can't. But...be careful."

"I will." He scuffed his feet into his shoes, then bent and kissed her hard on the lips. She clung to him, and it took all his willpower not to climb back into bed and spend the rest of the day making love to her while the storm raged outside.

He found a crew member in the galley making coffee,

and accepted a cup, then borrowed rain gear and headed up top. On deck the rain lashed at him, coming at him sideways and stinging like needles against his face. Another crew member helped him board the Zodiac. Fighting wind and high waves, he headed out to open seas.

He quickly decided not to try for his yacht but to head straight to the *Caspian*. Roger greeted him as he climbed aboard. "What are you doing here?" the older man shouted over the roar of wind and rain.

"I came to make sure everything's all right."

"It's not, but there's nothing we can do about it now."

He turned and headed toward the ship's main work room and Adam followed. "What's wrong?" he asked when they were inside.

Just then, Brent swung down the passage toward them on crutches, followed by Charlie and Tessa. "What happened to you?" Adam asked.

Brent looked sheepish. "We were securing the Zodiac and a rope snapped loose and whipped back on me." He looked down at his right leg, which was in an air cast. "I got a pretty good cut and bruise, but I don't think it's broken. At least, not much."

Adam frowned. "You won't be diving for a while with that. When the weather clears, I'll send you back to the States."

"No! I'm fine, really. And I can still help on deck and with cataloging the collection."

"There is no collection yet." Merrick joined them. He wore faded jeans and a pale blue sweatshirt and deck shoes, but his perfectly styled hair, Rolex watch and diamond-studded ring spoiled his attempt to pass as an ordinary sailor. Sandra might as well try to pass herself off as a milkmaid.

"We all know your opinion, so we don't need to hear it again," Adam said.

"How long before this passes over?" Merrick asked. "How soon can we dive again? Did you plan for this kind of thing in your original schedule?"

Did the man never shut up? Adam tossed his wet slicker and pants over the back of a chair.

"We'll use the time to do other things."

"Such as?" Merrick asked.

"Such as organizing the artifacts we have brought up, working on the desalination, cleaning and repairing our equipment."

"The winch needs repairing." Sam spoke from a table across the room where he sat nursing a coffee cup.

"When did it break?" Adam asked.

"Last night," Sam answered. "I stopped by your yacht to tell you, but you weren't there."

"Maybe there's something to this curse," Charlie said, before Adam could think of a plausible excuse for his absence from the yacht. "Everyone who's tried to live on the island or uncover the treasure has met with a bad end."

"You know I don't believe in that nonsense," Adam said.

Charlie pulled a chair from the table and pointedly set it next to Tessa. "We sure are snakebit all of a sudden."

"Maybe it means we're close to finding the treasure." Tessa scooted her chair over, closer to Brent.

"Or it could just be a run of bad luck," Charlie said.

Adam considered each of them, taking in Merrick's overeager handsomeness, the interns' youthful energy, and Sam's and Roger's grizzled skepticism. "I don't believe in luck, or curses," he said.

"You don't believe things happen for a reason?" Tessa asked.

"You mean, like fate?" Charlie grinned. "So you and I are working together on this project because we were fated to meet?"

She ignored him. "I think sometimes things happen for reasons we don't know," she said. "Maybe this storm came up so we'd have a day to work on our equipment."

"Then why was I hurt?" Brent asked.

"So she'd spend more time with me," Charlie said.

"I don't know," Tessa said. "That's the thing—we don't always know the reasons behind things happening, only that there is a reason."

Adam shook his head. "I believe things happen and there aren't always reasons," he said. "What matters is how you react. Having to take a day off or navigate around broken equipment or injuries doesn't matter. We're still going to keep working, and we're going to keep making progress."

Merrick opened his mouth to speak, but Adam cut him off. "You said you wanted to be part of the crew, so I have a job for you."

Merrick brightened. "What's that?"

"Help Charlie and Tessa with the desalination."

Merrick made a face, but said nothing. Adam turned to Brent. "I want you to work on making sure we have photographs and drawings of every item, along with a complete written description."

"I'm on it," Brent said.

"Sam and Charlie, do you need any help cleaning and prepping the equipment?" Adam asked.

"We'll let you know if we do," Charlie said.

"What are *you* going to do?" Merrick asked.

"I'm going to work on my report of what we've found so far," he said. And take a closer look at the charts and sonar images in the *Caspian*'s navigation room, to make sure he hadn't overlooked some anomaly that might point to *another* wreck in the same vicinity, in case the wreck they were diving really wasn't the *Eve*.

An hour later he'd pored over the charts and images and found nothing. He hadn't expected he would. He knew he'd found the *Eve,* though he couldn't explain why their search had yet to turn up anything of more than historical value.

Tessa would say there was a reason—and following that line of thinking, he supposed this meant that something besides his uncle's stories and an interest in historic artifacts had brought him to Passionata's Island. If a person believed in fate or destiny or whatever it was called, then he'd believe they were all on the island for some purpose.

He shook his head and returned to studying the charts. His only purpose here was to salvage the *Eve,* to fulfill his dream to bringing the past to light. He'd take home some great memories and a feeling of accomplishment, but he couldn't see that it would really change his life.

What about Sandra?

The thought stopped him. What about Sandra? Yes, she was an incredible woman and they'd had some great times together, but he'd known from the start they'd part company when the expedition was over. Yeah, he'd miss her. A lot. And maybe he wouldn't look at other women the same way after being with her. So that would be a change. But it wasn't as if he was in love with her or anything.

He crumpled the sheet of notes he'd made and clenched it tightly in his fist. Even if he was in love with her, it didn't matter. They were two people married to their careers. Trying to be a couple when they'd both been single so long was asking for trouble. Maybe some people were meant to be together for the rest of their lives, but he and Sandra obviously weren't like that. He wouldn't waste time wishing things were different. As Tessa might say, some things simply weren't meant to be.

12

BY THE NEXT DAY the weather had cleared and the team was able to resume diving. Adam was glad to see that the storm hadn't been fierce enough to disturb the grids they'd laid out, and only a few areas had filled with more sand. But as on previous days, they found nothing more exciting than a few iron nails and the broken hilt of a cutlass.

"This doesn't look as if it could have been shaped like a serpent, does it?" he asked, examining the tarnished and pitted silver of the cutlass's hilt. The team had gathered around the beachside worktable to review the day's haul.

Brent scrutinized the twisted metal and shook his head. "I don't think so. Why?"

"The poet John Dennis met Passionata and described her in a letter to a friend as wearing a cutlass that had a hilt shaped like a serpent, with ruby eyes. The blade was inscribed with the words *Passionata, Queen of the Pirates.*"

Brent whistled. "That would be a find."

"It would prove this wreck is the *Eve,*" Tessa said.

"She's beautiful *and* brilliant." Charlie winked at Tessa across the table. She shoved back her chair and excused herself.

"Why don't you leave her alone," Brent said, scowling at his fellow intern.

"Why don't we all keep our minds on *work.*" Adam

leaned over a chart of the debris field. The drawing was marked to indicate every item found so far, as well as magnetometer readings from their initial survey. "We got some strong readings in this area," he said, pointing to the easternmost section of the chart. "I believe this corresponds to the prow of the vessel. I want to start excavating there tomorrow, searching for the contents of the forward hold."

"We've already been over those areas," Sam said.

"Yes, but I want to dig deeper this time." He was playing a hunch, one he hoped would pay off.

"Do you think that's where the treasure was stored?" Merrick asked.

"I don't know what was stored there," Adam said. "I want to find out."

"There's something odd about this whole setup," Roger said, pointing a stubby finger at the map.

Adam stiffened. "What's that?"

"The *Eve* was a galley, right?"

Adam nodded.

"Then I'd expect to see more than we're getting—a bigger debris field, more artifacts."

This problem had nagged at Adam, as well. Was this proof they had the wrong ship? "What are you suggesting?"

"I think maybe the ship broke up before sinking. We're looking at part of it, but somewhere on the ocean floor is the rest of it."

"Is that why we haven't found any treasure?" Merrick asked. "Because it's with the rest of the ship?"

Roger shrugged. "I'm only guessing."

"It's certainly possible," Adam said. "The report of *Passionata*'s capture describes the British firing their cannon at the *Eve* at close range. That would be enough to split the vessel in two."

"Then why are we wasting our time excavating this section?" Merrick asked. "Why aren't we searching for the rest of the ship?"

Adam had grown so used to Merrick's outbursts that he no longer reacted to them. He kept his attention on Roger and the chart. "It would be worthwhile launching another expedition next summer to investigate the possibility of a second wreck site," he said. "Meanwhile, let's hope this forward hold section yields something of interest."

"I don't know why we can't look for the other section of the ship now," Merrick said. Everyone ignored him. Abandoning the salvage effort at this point to go in search of a separate wreck site would waste valuable time. They had to return to the United States by the end of August, which left only a few more weeks to retrieve all they could from the site they'd already devoted so much effort to plotting and photographing.

Merrick rose and began to pace around the table.

"Sit down," Adam said. He handed the billionaire an encrusted iron bar. "Measure that, sketch it and weigh it."

Merrick looked at the bar, turning it over and over in his hand, then returned to his seat and began making a credible sketch. Maybe that was the key to dealing with him, Adam thought. Give him something to do.

Keeping him busy also served to prevent him from stalking Sandra. In addition to his constant dinner invitations, Merrick had taken to sticking close to her whenever she was near the team. Her polite but frosty response never deterred him.

Adam looked down the beach to where Sandra reclined on a beach chair in the shade of a large umbrella. She scribbled something on a yellow legal pad in her lap, hard at work like the rest of them. But more than a strip of sand separated her from Adam and the rest. While they huddled beneath the crude shelter they'd made themselves, drinking tepid water from canteens brought from the ship and nibbling on hastily assembled ham sandwiches, Sandra had a steward who fetched bottles of sparkling water, plates of fresh fruit and cheese, fresh towels and a fan. She might have been relaxing poolside in Cannes, rather than on a remote, uninhabited island.

Watching her now, Adam felt the difference between them keenly. They might be compatible in the bedroom, but what would a television glamour gal and a history professor from Ann Arbor have in common back in the real world? Her first faculty dinner would bore her to tears, and her television cronies would take one look at his worn shoes and hair in need of a trim and laugh her out of the room.

He forced his gaze away, back to the chart in front of him. Uncle Benny had once advised him that women were like expensive orchids—nice to look at and smell, but more trouble than they were worth to keep around. Just as well his prospects of keeping Sandra were slim to none. She wasn't the kind of woman any man would keep. The best he could hope for was that they'd still be friends when this trip was over. They'd have their work to keep them busy and nice memories to look back on, and no messy complications to disturb their peace. Exactly the way he'd always thought life should be.

"SANDRA, DO YOU HAVE a minute to talk?"

Sandra looked up at Tessa. She'd been working on notes for her documentary script when the intern approached her beach chair.

"Sure, have a seat." Sandra indicated the empty chair beside her. "What's up?"

"I need your help." Tessa sat and looked around, as if to make sure they were alone, then leaned toward Sandra. "It's Charlie," she said. "He won't leave me alone."

"I assume you've tried telling him to get lost."

"He won't take no for an answer." Worry lines creased her forehead. "He told me one of his defining characteristics is persistence, and it's always paid off for him."

Sandra made a face. "Nice of him to consider *your* feelings. What can I do to help?"

"I was hoping you knew some way I could get rid of him."

"So you could spend more time with Brent?" Sandra asked. She'd noticed the pretty intern seemed to gravitate to the dark-haired young man.

Tessa blushed. "Well…yeah. I really like him, and I think he likes me, too, but we're never alone enough for me to find out." She rolled her eyes. "I thought I'd be past all this high-school stuff by now."

"In some ways it never ends," Sandra said. She set aside her notepad. "Frankly, I'd like to find a way to tell Damian Merrick to get lost and have him believe I mean it." The billionaire's attentions were not only annoying, they were making it more and more difficult for her to sneak off to be with Adam.

"I know it's none of my business, but is there something going on between you and the professor?" Tessa asked.

Sandra looked away. "What makes you think that?" she asked warily.

"I've noticed the way he looks at you, and you both seem to disappear at the same time…" She shrugged. "Don't worry, I won't say anything if you want to keep it a secret."

Sandra crossed her legs and feigned nonchalance. "Adam and I enjoy each other's company," she said. "We have fun together." Which was true. For a man who could be as intense about his work as she was about hers, the two of them were able to let down their hair around each other. They were good for each other.

"That's nice," Tessa said. "I imagine spending the whole summer in this isolated place is hard for someone like you."

"What do you mean?"

"Well, you're used to being in the spotlight, aren't you? Going out to clubs and to parties and things like that. All this—" she indicated the empty beach and still water "—must be really boring for you."

Sandra laughed. "The one thing I haven't been, here on Passionata's Island, is bored." Which was odd, really. She *was* used to a much more active social life. But she liked most of the members of this expedition, and she felt comfortable in this setting, more at home, in fact, than she had anywhere in years, or possibly ever.

And while she wouldn't say she *needed* to be in the spotlight all the time, she accepted fame as a necessity for success in her chosen career. If people forgot about her, her career would be over.

The thought reminded her of the gamble she was taking, spending the summer out of the public eye. But she was counting on this documentary to catapult her to an even higher level of success. This project, if successful, would make it tougher for her bosses to dismiss her as just another pretty woman.

"It's nice to take a break," she said. "And I'm enjoying the work I'm doing, and all of you."

"And Professor Carroway," Tessa teased.

She laughed. "Yes, him, too. And I'd enjoy him more if I could get Damian out of the way."

"Yeah." Tessa sat back in the chair and sighed. "Here I thought I had the perfect summer planned, essentially stranded on a desert island with a guy I want—and the guy I *don't* want is ruining it."

"Yeah, if only we could strand *them* on an island away from us." Sandra stared out at the ocean. The sky was so blue, the surface of the water so calm, it was difficult to believe Roger's prediction of more bad weather to come. The air was so clear she could make out the line of small atolls off Passionata Island's western shore, like beads decorating the hem of a woman's skirt.

She sat up straight, inspiration blossoming. "I have an idea," she said, grinning.

"A way to get Charlie and Mr. Merrick out of our hair?"

Sandra nodded. "I think it might work, if you feel up to a little playacting."

"I was in the drama club in high school."

"Then I'd say the two of us are just the women to pull this off."

THE TEAM HAD SETTLED into a routine of diving in the morning and spending the afternoons cataloging the day's finds, repairing equipment and seeing to housekeeping tasks. Though part of the work had to be carried out on board the *Caspian,* they'd set up a second workshop under a large canopy on the beach facing the bay. Here they could spread out and take a break from the close confines of the ship.

The next afternoon Sandra showed up on the beach wearing her briefest bikini beneath a sheer cover-up. Tessa met her wearing a less-revealing tankini. Sandra carried a tote bag from which protruded the top of a large wine bottle and the handle of a beach umbrella.

"Tessa and I thought we'd spend the afternoon exploring the string of atolls on the west side of the island," Sandra announced to the men assembled around the tables set up beneath the canopy.

Adam frowned and started to say something, but Merrick cut him off. "That's an excellent idea," he said, standing and walking over to the women. "But you shouldn't venture over there alone. I'll go with you."

"I'll go, too," Charlie announced, abandoning the chart on which he'd been entering GPS coordinates of artifacts they'd found so far—part of a pistol, cannonballs, bottles and broken pottery, but no more gold or silver or jewels.

"You have work to do." Adam shoved back his chair and stood. "And so does Tessa."

"Even indentured servants in the 1700s got a half day off," Sandra said, smiling sweetly, though her eyes sent the message that he should stay out of this. "Tessa and I need a little girl time."

"Then Merrick and Charlie don't need to go along," Adam said.

"I really think they should go," Tessa said. "We don't know what we might find on the atolls." She gave Charlie a dazzling smile. "I'd feel better with a man along."

Brent looked sick to his stomach as he watched Charlie and Tessa's exchange. Sandra almost felt sorry for him. Then again, jealousy could be a powerful motivator. Maybe if Charlie were pigheaded enough to continue to pursue Tessa after today, Brent would find the balls to tell him to get lost.

Come to think of it, Adam looked as if he'd swallowed something that tasted bad. But Sandra gave him points for not interfering. "You'll need one of the Zodiacs," he said, his voice strained.

"Oh, no, we won't," Sandra said. "The tide's down. We can walk over."

"But when the tide comes in…" Brent protested.

"We'll be *fine*," Sandra said, giving him a hard look. "We're only going to walk around a little bit."

Adam stared at the tote bag with the bottle of wine and umbrella while Sandra silently pleaded with him to keep his mouth shut. Now was not the time for him to go all macho and overprotective on her.

He sat, though one hand continued to grip the table edge, white-knuckled. "If you're not back by four o'clock, I'll send someone out to look for you."

"We'd appreciate that," Sandra said, and turned to leave before he could say anything more.

"Maybe we should take the Zodiac," Charlie said. "We can motor around to the back side of the atolls. The tide comes in pretty suddenly around here."

"The whole point of this expedition is that we want to walk," Tessa said.

"That's right," Sandra agreed. "If you don't want to come with us, you don't have to." She smiled at her partner in crime. "Tessa and I will just have to drink this wine all by ourselves."

"Yes, and we'll just have to rub suntan lotion on each other instead of having you help," Tessa added.

Charlie's eyes actually bugged out a little as he apparently pictured the two of them slathering each other in suntan oil, and Sandra had to turn away to contain her laughter. Sometimes men—at least some men—were so predictable.

As soon as they were out of sight of the work tent, she slipped off her cover-up and stuffed it into her bag. The sun warmed her skin and the sand was hot between her toes. If not for the company she was in, it would have been a perfect day. As soon as she got rid of Merrick, maybe she could persuade Adam to sneak away with her. She could pack a picnic and some blankets. Maybe while they were on the atoll she'd scout out a suitably private location....

"You're absolutely gorgeous," Merrick interrupted her thoughts as he moved in closer. "Your beauty is wasted on this bunch of eggheads. Good thing I decided to come along on the expedition."

"Hmm." She managed not to flinch as he put his arm around her.

"When we reach the atoll, we should find a way to lose these kids and spend some time alone," he said.

"Now that's an idea." She looked up at Tessa, who was walking with Charlie a little way ahead of them. Tessa smiled awkwardly at Charlie while he waved his arms and expounded on some subject. Perhaps he was telling her again of his many "defining" qualities.

At the western end of Passionata's Island, they waded through shallow water to the first atoll. The rocky islet was about the size of a football field, coconut palms huddled together in the middle like the topknot on a bald baby's head.

"Let's walk farther out, to one of the bigger atolls," Tessa said. "It doesn't look like there's anywhere comfortable to spread out here."

"Yes, this one doesn't really offer enough privacy," Sandra said with a coy look directed at Merrick.

"Keep your eye out for sharks," Charlie said as they stepped into the water once more.

"Sharks!" Tessa glared at him. "This water isn't deep enough for sharks."

"Actually, the little black-tipped sharks will come up in these shallows if they think there's easy prey," he said. "They've been known to take off a person's foot."

"You're just trying to frighten us," Sandra said, looking

around nervously. The water was up past their knees even with the tide at its lowest point.

"If you don't believe me, look there." Charlie pointed to a sleek shadow a short distance away. It turned to swim toward them, and Sandra saw the familiar sinister grin of the ocean's most feared predator, even if this one was a miniature model.

Tessa squealed and jumped back. "Don't worry," Charlie said. "I'll carry you across." Before she could protest, he gathered her into his arms.

Tessa looked back over his shoulder at Sandra, her expression miserable. "I hate sharks," she said, as Charlie strode forward.

"Allow me." Merrick held out his arms and made as if to scoop up Sandra.

"No, thanks," she said, and took the beach umbrella from her bag. "If any of those toothy midgets head my way, I'll bash its head in." Better a finned shark than the two-legged kind. Not to mention she had a firm policy of never playing the helpless female.

The second atoll was larger, but even rockier than the first. "I know it sounds like Goldilocks, but why don't we try the third one?" Sandra said. "From here it appears to be the largest, and I think I even see a bit of a sandy beach near those trees."

"Why not?" Merrick said. "This way we can say we explored all of them, and that one looks large enough to have some interesting places we can investigate on our own." He winked at her.

Again Charlie insisted on carrying Tessa across. Sandra noted with satisfaction that he was breathing hard by the time they reached the island, sweat running down his back. Tessa was a tall girl with healthy curves.

Once on land, Sandra set up her beach umbrella and Tessa spread a blanket.

"Let's have that wine," Charlie said.

"Not yet," Sandra said. "I want to get some sun." She lay back on the blanket and closed her eyes.

"Let me rub some sunscreen on you," Merrick said. "We wouldn't want that pretty skin to burn."

Sandra struggled not to make a face. "I'm fine," she said. "I put some on before I left my boat."

Merrick fell silent. He sat on the blanket beside her, then stood and began to pace. "Why don't we take a walk?" he asked.

Sandra sighed and lifted her head enough to check the tide. It was slightly higher than before, but not high enough to prevent the men from walking back to the island. She had to keep Merrick occupied a while longer. And getting him away from shore was probably a good idea.

She sat up. "All right," she said. "Let's take a walk." She looked at Tessa, who was talking with Charlie. He was drawing diagrams in the sand—maybe something to do with their work. "Damian and I are going to do some exploring," she said.

They set off, picking their way through the trees. "At least this place isn't overrun with birds," Sandra said.

"Did you know the Brits had planned to build an air base here not too long ago?" Merrick said.

"I heard something about it when I was here last summer." At the time, a man named Ian Marshall had been living on the island, documenting the plant and animal life on behalf of an environmental group who wanted to stop construction of the airbase. "I gave some film that I took to a man who hoped to use it for a campaign to save the island," she said.

"I don't know if it was your film or the discovery of the treasure, but the plans have been put on hold for now." Merrick held back a palm frond that blocked the path and allowed her to pass.

Despite the shade, in the still confines of the jungle the air was close and hot. Sandra twisted her hair in a knot off her neck. "How do you know all this?" she asked.

"I did my homework," he said. "If I was going to invest in this treasure hunt, I didn't want it called off in the middle so the bulldozers could move in. And I didn't want the Brits claiming a share of the treasure."

She whirled to face him. "Can they do that?"

"They could, but as it happens, the wreck is just outside the limit of their boundary waters, so we're in the clear. Unless they decide to sue, which could happen, but it's a suit we'd win—eventually."

Her reporter's instincts couldn't resist knowing more. Much as Merrick annoyed her, she also found him intriguing. "Why *did* you decide to invest in this expedition?" she asked.

He glanced at her, his expression guarded. "What do you see when you look at me?" he asked.

"What? Is this some kind of quiz?"

"I want to know your opinion of me—honestly."

She pressed her lips together. Honesty was a tricky business. In her experience, most of the time when people insisted they wanted you to be honest with them, they never liked what you said. "I see a rich, handsome man who has everything going for him. And," she added, going for broke. "I see a man who uses his money and position to keep people at arm's length."

To her surprise, the answer made him smile. "Instead of paying my therapist for years, I should have simply contacted you."

"That still doesn't tell me why you decided to back this expedition," she said.

He let out a heavy breath. "When Professor Carroway pitched his idea, I was intrigued by the story and the romance of sunken treasure and all that, of course, but also by the idea of a small group of people spending a summer together on a deserted island." His eyes met hers once more, stripped of their arrogance, startlingly vulnerable. "I wanted to be a part of that group. I wanted to be the reason they were even together."

"You wanted to make friends?" she asked, unsure if that was what he meant.

He nodded. "Friends. And…and I wanted them to look up to me."

The simpleness of this wish, and the ham-handed way he'd gone about trying to make it come true, touched her. She cleared her throat, considering her words. "I think you *are* a man other people could look up to," she said. "You have money and looks, which is always a good start. And you're willing to work for what you want." No one could charge Merrick hadn't done his fair share of labor on this trip.

"But…" he said. "I know there's a *but* on the end of that sentence, implied if not stated."

She nodded. "*But* you're never going to make people like you if you keep interjecting your own opinion and overruling their ideas."

His face flushed. "I don't do that. Do I?"

"You do. You do it every time you object to the way Professor Carroway is running things. Every time you urge him to neglect the proper research and move faster."

"The man is so plodding. It drives me crazy."

"He's doing his job." She spoke more sharply than she'd intended. "From what I've seen, he does it well. Scientific study isn't a timed race. It's important to lay a good foundation and establish facts that can't be refuted later."

Merrick grunted. "I guess I'm not used to taking orders from anyone."

"That's part of being on a team," she said gently. "There's only one leader, and in this case it's the professor. He hired all the other members, so they're going to take his side most of the time. If you really want to be included as one of them, you're going to have to learn when to listen instead of talk."

He nodded. "What about you? You're not part of the team, are you?"

She shook her head. "Like you, I—or rather, my station—invested money in the expedition so that I could make my documentary. The professor wasn't very happy about that, but he's a practical man, and I think he's accepted my presence here."

Merrick snorted. "I've seen the way he watches you. Believe me, he's not complaining."

This was the second time in two days someone had mentioned the way Adam watched her. "What do you mean?" she asked. "How does he look at me?"

"The same way I look at you. With good, old-fashioned lust. Frankly, I didn't know the professor had it in him. I guess even academic types enjoy the sins of the flesh."

"Just what I always wanted to be, a sex object." She turned around. "I'm ready to head back to the others."

"I don't see you *only* as a sex object," Merrick protested as they started toward the beach. "You're obviously a very talented, intelligent woman. One who's accustomed to the finer things in life. The two of us have more in common than anyone else on the island."

What would Merrick say if he knew the smart, sophisticated woman before him had been born Sandy Day in Oil Patch, Oklahoma, daughter of an alcoholic ex-con and his chronically depressed wife; older sister to three younger siblings, every one of whom she'd supported at one time or another with money earned from her television career, beginning with her stint as weather girl on KSWO in Oilton, Oklahoma.

Merrick might have ambitions to be friends with the common people, but she'd spent the past twenty years struggling not to *be* one of them. Common, that is. As in her grandmother's definition. Being *common* to Grandmother Day meant a person had loose morals and little sense of decency. It was common for her youngest son, Sandy's father, to drink up his check from the oil company and come home and hit his wife. It was common for him to be a manual laborer to begin with, considering his parents had done everything in their power to provide him with a good education, an effort he rejected when he quit school at fifteen to work in the oil fields.

Which left Sandy to try to live up to her grandmother's dreams of what was respectable. Appearing on television wearing an expensive suit, hair and nails styled to perfection, counted for a lot in her Grandmother's book, as did having the money to pay for her siblings' education and to give her parents grand funerals when they finally drank themselves to death.

Being kicked out of the business for wasting the station's money would be common and disgraceful, as was any kind of failure in her grandmother's book. Sandy wasn't allowed to fail. The whipping she'd gotten the first—and last—time she brought home a D on her report card proved that.

The globe charm necklace hadn't only been an endorsement of Sandra's dreams for the future. It had been an affirmation that Grandmother Day *expected* great things from her eldest grandchild.

Why she was thinking about all this now, Sandra couldn't say. Except that her grandmother probably would have liked Damian Merrick. The man reeked of material success, and Grandmother Day had always appreciated arrogance in a man she felt deserved to be arrogant.

When they emerged from the jungle onto the beach once more, she was relieved to see that the tide had risen, waves hitting the rocks and sending up spray onto the considerably narrower stretch of sand. Charlie and Tessa were lying side by side on the blanket, eyes closed, though as Sandra and Merrick approached, Tessa sat up.

"Why don't you fellows open the wine while Tessa and I freshen up?" Sandra said.

"Freshen up?" Charlie rolled onto his side and propped himself on one elbow. "Is that chick-speak for taking a leak?"

"You don't have to be crude," Tessa scolded. She linked her arm with Sandra's. "We'll be back in a little bit. Save some wine for us."

"Hey, there are only two glasses," Charlie protested as he dug into Sandra's tote bag.

"I guess we'll have to share," Sandra called over her shoulder.

13

ONCE THEY WERE HIDDEN by the trees, the two women ran toward the opposite side of the atoll, where they pulled a dinghy from the hiding place they'd stashed it in when they rowed over the previous evening.

They climbed in and rowed out to deeper water before firing up the motor. Sandra steered around toward the front of the atoll, until they were within sight of the two men, who sat side by side on the blankets.

"Hope you enjoy the wine, boys!" she shouted, waving.

Both men leaped to their feet, shouting protests. The women waved and, laughing, gunned the motor and headed toward Sandra's yacht.

"What do you think they'll do now?" Tessa asked.

"They could try to swim to the island, but it's a long way."

Tessa shuddered. "I wouldn't want to risk it with the sharks. Maybe we should send someone after them."

"They only have to wait twelve hours and they can walk back," Sandra said. "There's food in my tote bag, along with water, sunblock and the wine. They'll be fine."

"They'll be *furious*," Tessa said.

"Serves them right." She deepened her voice. "'Watch out for sharks. Tessa, I'll carry you,'" she mimicked. "Talk about a lame excuse to feel you up."

"It was a tough choice," Tessa conceded. "But I really

hate sharks. Have you seen the scar on the professor's leg?"

Sandra smiled. "I've seen it. Up close and personal."

Tessa laughed. Then her expression sobered. "Do you think this will work? Do you think they'll leave us alone now?"

"They're both intelligent men," Sandra said. She thought back to her conversation with Merrick. He knew more than he let on sometimes. "We've made them look foolish, which they won't like. They won't want to give us another opportunity."

"At least now Brent and I will have a chance to get to know each other better and see where things go from here."

"I hope it works out for you," Sandra said.

"Me, too. We have so much in common and I'm ready to settle down, you know? We'll both be eligible for teaching positions next year. I think it would be a good time to start a family."

Sandra studied the young woman. Tessa was at least ten years younger than Sandra, and yet she had her whole future figured out. Her determination was frightening, really.

"You've got plenty of time," Sandra said. "No need to rush into anything."

"I don't feel like I'm rushing," Tessa said. "I mean, I love my work and want to continue doing it, but I want more. I want a good man to come home to, and children. I guess that seems old-fashioned to someone like you, who doesn't need those things."

"I never said I don't need those things," Sandra said quickly. But it had been many years since she'd allowed herself to think of them. She'd practically raised her brothers and sister, then had devoted herself to getting ahead in her career. After so many years of being tied down by other commitments, she'd enjoyed savoring the freedom she'd earned.

"Maybe you're just waiting on the right man," Tessa said. "You'll know him when you meet him, I think."

Would she? Sandra had dated a lot of men over the years, some of whom were still friends, others with whom things had ended badly when she'd refused to conform to their ideas of the perfect partner. She'd been attracted to strong, independent types, only to have them balk at her own strength and independence. She'd sought comfort from more passive men, but soon grew bored with their passivity.

Adam was strong and independent, also smart and funny, and definitely not passive. So far he seemed to admire her attitude toward life and respect her career, but they really hadn't been together long enough to know for sure.

What was she saying? They hadn't been *together* really at all. Add to that the disturbing spells she'd suffered several times in his presence, and how could she believe anything lasting would come of this island interlude?

But listening to Tessa talk of her dreams of happily ever after with Brent, Sandra realized she really *wanted* that kind of happiness for herself.

And a small voice inside of her she could no longer ignore said she wanted it with Adam.

SANDRA AND HER CAMERAMAN joined Adam, Tessa and Roger for the first dive the next day. "You'll need to stay back," Adam told them as they prepared for the dive. "We're using the water dredge to suck up the sand and there could be a lot of debris floating around. I can't promise you'll get any good film."

"You never know if the footage you shot in a day is any good until you look at it later," Sandra said. After her triumph with Merrick yesterday, she was in high spirits. "If I get in your way, just tell me."

"Don't make her mad, Professor," Roger said. "She might try to maroon you on a deserted island."

True to his promise, Adam had sent a search party consisting of Sam and Brent to the atolls shortly after four the previous afternoon. They'd found an angry and embarrassed Merrick and Charlie, and no sign of the women.

The next Sandra had seen of them was when the rescue mission detoured to her yacht, where she and Tessa were drinking margaritas and giving each other pedicures. "We were tired of you and Charlie bugging us and wanted to teach you a lesson," she'd explained when Merrick complained about being left on the island, and none of the men had the balls to argue with her.

Merrick and Charlie had been subdued this morning, keeping their distance from the two women and happy to help with the diving and dredging equipment.

"I have a good feeling about today," she said to Adam as he helped her with her air tanks. "I think you're going to find something good today."

"I hope you're right," he said, then left to don his own gear.

She gave him a sympathetic look. Everything they'd both worked so hard for depended upon Adam and his team locating more than the handful of gold coins and dented artifacts they'd found so far. If they found treasure, they'd be heroes. But if they continued to come up empty-handed, they'd go home in a few weeks defeated.

"Everybody ready?" he asked, fitting his mask over his eyes. "Let's go." He fell back into the water. Sandra followed him down toward the wreck site, the others trailing behind. They descended slowly, sunlight giving way to dimness, the water cooling with each meter's descent, the only sound the hollow roar of her own breathing filling her ears.

When they reached the site, Adam indicated the grid where they were to dig, and Roger and Tessa manipulated the water dredge over it. Water pumped into the dredge created suction, allowing the dredge to vacuum up great quantities of sand, clearing the way for deeper exploration. The ocean clouded, then cleared as the loose sand was moved away. Sandra switched on her headlamp and swam closer, until she hovered just behind Adam's shoulder. Dark lumps began to appear in the grid, and he used his hand to clear away more sand. The lumps became the top of a dented trunk, the bands holding it together black with rust.

Sandra's heart pounded as Jonas moved in for a closer shot. Adam reached for the lid of the trunk and it disintegrated in his hand. For a moment their view was obscured by a fog of black silt.

Sandra knew what would be inside the trunk even before the fog cleared. She knew it with the certainty she knew her mother's face. She signaled Jonas to focus the camera in closer, zeroing in on gleaming piles of gold coins.

Adam threw his arms in the air in a gesture of triumph, then hugged her tightly to him. Relief flooded her; they hadn't failed. She felt like shouting or weeping, but could only grin at Adam, who grinned back and continued to hold her tightly against him.

Looking at him, her vision fogged, then shimmered. She blinked, but he seemed not to notice, and turned toward the treasure. She wiped at her goggles, wondering what had obscured them. She felt light-headed and quickly checked her gauges, but her oxygen levels were fine.

Adam was too involved with the treasure to notice her discomfort. She gritted her teeth and watched as he moved

to the next grid, hurrying now, digging quickly and carefully and unearthing one find after another. Jonas hurried
to keep up with him, the camera recording each new discovery: a blackened heap that turned out to be silver bars,
a set of jeweled cups made of gold, another chest of coins
and a third filled with painted porcelain.

Sandra hung back, and stared at it all with an overwhelming sense of déjà vu. She felt disembodied, floating
somewhere above the scene, like a spectator watching a
familiar movie. When Adam signaled they should head to
the surface, she turned to lead the way, but was unable to
move, as if something physically held her in place.

Without realizing how it happened, she saw herself pointing, then nudging Adam toward a section of the grid fifty feet
from where they'd focused the morning's search. He gave her
a curious look, then shrugged and swam to that area. She
followed, Jonas trailing them with his camera. She could no
longer control the pounding of her heart, and she breathed
heavily, consumed by an almost uncontrollable excitement.

Adam indicated Tessa and Roger should direct the water
dredge to the grid Sandra indicated. As they sucked away
the layers of sand, it appeared at first as if there was nothing
of interest here, only bits of corroded iron and some broken
wine bottles. Adam shook his head, but Sandra pushed him
away impatiently and began digging with her own hands,
until her knuckles scraped against something hard. She
dug faster, and revealed a rusty iron square amid the sand.

She reached out to tug at the cover, but he put out a hand
to stop her. Only then did she realize how jagged the metal
was; it surely would have cut her.

Adam looked around, then swam a short distance away
and returned with an iron bar. Though rusty, it was still largely
intact. He used this to carefully pry the lid from the box.

Heads close together to peer into the box, they looked down on an object nestled in some kind of cloth, glinting with jewels and the gleam of gold.

Adam retrieved the item and examined it. It was a box, about the size of a small loaf of bread, enamel and gold, studded with jewels. He handed it to Sandra. She turned it over and over, admiring the enameled portrait of a lady in court dress that adorned the top, the woman's gown and headdress studded with rubies, sapphires and rose-cut diamonds.

Dizziness overtook her once more as she stared at the portrait. For a split second she wasn't floating on the bottom of the ocean, but standing in a fancy shop in London, an unctuous clerk hovering at her elbow while a big blond man dressed in a knee-length red coat trimmed in gold braid, a cascade of white ruffles at his throat, smiled indulgently at her.

"Frederick," she gasped, and fainted dead away.

ADAM WATCHED IN ALARM as Sandra's eyes fluttered and she slumped forward, the jeweled casket floating from her hand. He pulled her to him and checked her gauges. They were fine, and he was relieved to discover she was still breathing, but she was out cold. The others gathered around, gesturing and waving, silently demanding to know what was wrong. Ignoring them, he cradled Sandra close and started for the surface.

He carried her limp body with him to the first rest point. She was still breathing, though shallowly, but her face was as pale as milk, and her pulse fluttered wildly beneath his fingers.

On the slow ascent, her eyes began to flutter. He patted her arm in what he hoped was a soothing gesture. Tessa swam beside him, helping him to support Sandra's body.

He checked his watch, cursing the necessity of ascending so slowly. But a case of the bends wouldn't do any of them any good.

By the time they surfaced, Sandra had raised her head and was looking around, though she made no attempt to move from his arms. Charlie met them at the side of the dive boat and helped to haul her aboard. "What happened?" he asked as Adam fell into the boat beside the reporter.

"Did you find anything down there?" Merrick loomed over Adam, his tone demanding and impatient.

Adam helped Sandra remove her tanks, mask and flippers. "Are you okay?" he asked, caressing her shoulder. "What happened?"

She shook her head. "I don't know," she said, her voice faint. She accepted a bottle of water from Charlie and took a long drink. "I was staring at the jewelry box, and then I fainted."

"Jewelry box? What jewelry box?" Merrick knelt in front of them.

"Is this what she's talking about?" Jonas held out the enameled casket. In the sunlight the colors of the enamel were brilliant reds, blues and greens, the gold a rich metallic yellow that could be duplicated by nothing but the purest ore. The woman in the painting on the top smiled coyly at them, the jewels of her dress glittering.

"Where did you find that?" Merrick snatched for the casket, but Charlie was faster.

"It'll need to go into a desalination tank right away," he said. "If the sun dries it out, the salt could crack that enamel and it'll be worthless."

Adam gave him a grateful look. "Take care of it for me, will you, Charlie? And have Brent enter it into the inventory right away, as well." He turned back to Sandra. "Are you sure you're all right?" he asked. "Do you think you're coming down with something?"

"You're not pregnant, are you?" Roger asked.

Color flooded her cheeks, at the same time it drained from Adam's. "No, I'm not pregnant," she said. "I just…I think in the excitement I must have hyperventilated."

Her gaze flickered to Adam and in that moment he knew she was lying. This had something to do with the other strange spells she'd had, he was sure, but this was not the time or place to pursue the subject further. He patted her shoulder, then turned toward Jonas. "Did you get some good footage?"

The camera man grinned and patted the camera. "I got some great stuff—the gold, the silver—all of it."

"Gold? Silver?" Merrick was practically shouting now, his face flushed. "Show me," he demanded. Then, not waiting for an answer, he moved to a set of tanks and prepared to put them on. "Better yet, I'll go down and see for myself."

Adam's hand closed around his wrist. "You know the rules. No one goes down without another member of the team."

"I'll take Charlie down with me." Merrick shrugged out of Adam's grasp and picked up a weight belt.

"No," Adam said. "No one is going down until we've discussed this. We'll go back to the *Caspian* and look at the footage Jonas shot, then make a plan to retrieve everything in an orderly, scientific manner."

Merrick started to argue, the struggle evident on his face. Then he took a deep breath and let the tanks slide to the bottom of the boat. "All right. But I want to go on the second dive this afternoon."

"You're welcome to come," Adam said, feeling gracious in the face of Merrick's restraint. Was it possible those few hours stranded on the atoll had resulted in an attitude shift? He turned to Roger. "Let's get back to the ship."

He settled down next to Sandra as Roger fired up the dive boat's engine and they started toward the *Caspian*. She was still pale, but her eyes held more life. He took her hand under the pretense of checking her pulse. To his relief, it was strong, if a little fast. "So you think that was a jewel chest?" he asked casually.

She nodded. "Yes. Inside is a removable tray and compartments for bracelets, rings and earrings."

He looked at her sharply. "We didn't open it yet."

Her expression clouded. "We didn't? But I could have sworn…" Her voice faded and she shook her head.

Jonas crouched in front of him. "How you doing, boss?" he asked.

She managed a smile. "I'm fine. Sorry if I scared you."

"That's a pretty box you found," Jonas said. "Looks like it might be worth a bit. How did you know it was in that particular grid?"

"I don't know." She looked away, obviously upset. Adam wondered again what had happened to her down there.

They reached the ship and were met at the rail by the rest of the team. "What did you find?" Brent asked.

Charlie handed him the cask. "There's more where this came from," he said.

They all gathered around to admire the delicate jeweled box. "It's gorgeous," Tessa enthused.

"Looks valuable," Brent said.

"Open it," Adam said.

"If I can do it without damaging it," Brent said. He felt along the rim of the casket until he found a catch. Carefully, he pried up the lid, revealing a blackened compartment filled with water.

"Ugh." He dumped stagnant seawater onto the deck. Then he carefully lifted out a disintegrating tray. "It feels like some kind of fabric, maybe velvet," he said. "In pretty sorry shape now." He peered into the casket and shook his head. "It's empty. Sorry."

"That's all right." Adam glanced at Sandra, who was avoiding meeting anyone's eyes. How had she known?

Charlie and Brent left to take the casket to the desalination tanks. "Tessa, tell everyone to meet in the work room in fifteen minutes," Adam said.

She hurried to do as he asked, leaving Adam and Sandra alone by the rail. "How are you feeling?" he asked. "Do you want me to have someone take you to your yacht so you can rest?"

She shook her head. "No, I'm fine. I want to see the footage Jonas shot."

He resisted the impulse to argue. "All right. I'm going to go find some coffee. I'll meet you there." Later they would talk and he would get to the bottom of whatever was happening to her.

AFTER A TRIP to the ladies' room to splash cold water on her face and try to collect herself, Sandra joined the others in the workroom. Jonas had set up a screen and a computer to play the footage he'd captured. Sandra took a seat at the far end of the table, as far from Adam as she could. She was aware of him watching her with an air of over-protectiveness she found both endearing and aggravating. Did he think she was crazy, liable to flake out again any minute?

She still didn't understand what had happened down

there. One minute she'd been fine, the next she'd been…someone else. And some*where* else. Was she hallucinating? How else to explain the vision in the London shop? But *why* was this happening to her? And why now?

Charlie dimmed the lights and Jonas started the film. A wide shot of the ocean and the debris field opened this series. The strange undersea world of starfish and sea anemones and colorful coral filled the screen. The camera panned over the rusted metal, broken bottles and barnacle-covered iron scattered across the debris field, then focused on Adam as he crouched on top of one of the orange-and-white grids, combing through the sand with his bare hands.

A swirl of orange rust filled the screen then, like a genie's treasure conjured in a puff of smoke, Adam's hand appeared, filled with gleaming gold coins.

The crew, silent until now, erupted into applause and cheers, and all began talking at once. "How much do you think is down there?"

"Are those Spanish doubloons or English sovereigns?"

"Is there just the one chest, or more?"

"Keep watching," Adam said, and nodded toward the screen.

They fell silent again as the screen filled with the image of a pile of what looked at first to be blacked bricks. Adam hefted one in two hands, then balanced it against his knee and scraped at the surface with his diving knife. Bright silver gleamed through the black.

"Silver ingots," Brent said in a reverent tone.

"There looks to be about thirty in that pile," Charlie added.

"There are at least two other piles like that," Adam said.

"What are they, about fifty pounds each?" Merrick asked.

"They vary," Adam said. "It was customary for individuals to make their own bars, marked with their own insignia."

"It's a lot of silver, just the same," Roger said.

The scene shifted to a large trunk, which Adam and Sandra opened to reveal porcelain cups and saucers, the delicate painted china still intact after all these years.

"Dishes," Merrick said dismissively.

"Antique china and porcelain can be quite rare and valuable," Tessa said. "It could be worth more than that chest full of coins."

"You're kidding," Merrick said.

She shook her head. "I'm not. Those dishes could be the best find of all."

"No, I think this is the best find," Charlie said, as the camera showed another trunk, empty except for three gold goblets. The rim of each goblet was studded with a different precious stone—rubies on one, sapphires on another, emeralds on a third.

"Sweet!" Brent said, and the others laughed.

The film continued, showing Adam ready to leave, and Sandra urging him toward a new grid. The camera focused into the hole the water dredge dug, following the beam of Adam's flashlight, fixing on the rusty metal box. The crew watched, scarcely breathing, as Adam pried the lid from the box and lifted out the enameled casket.

Sandra studied her own face behind the diving mask. The glare of light and water made it impossible to see her eyes, but did she imagine the familiar, almost *possessive* way she held the delicate box?

A collective gasp sounded from the viewers as Sandra slumped against Adam, and the screen went black.

Everyone turned to look at her. "What happened?" Brent asked.

She shrugged. "I hyperventilated. Really, I'm fine. I feel stupid." She forced herself to smile and look unconcerned. "What we need to decide now is how to go about retrieving everything."

"Everything should be photographed *in situ* before we move anything," Adam said. "We really shouldn't have brought the casket up, but in the heat of the moment I wasn't thinking."

"Fine, take your photographs, then let's get everything up as quickly as possible," Merrick said. "No more wasting time."

"We'll have to bring everything up one or two items at a time," Adam continued. "We'll need to take extra care with the porcelain."

"I want to film it all," Sandra said. "A lot of the footage I won't use, but I can't say what I'll need for the final documentary until I've looked at everything."

"You should let Jonas do the filming," he said. "I don't want you diving again until we figure out why you fainted today."

"Jonas will film some, but I want to be there," she said. "I *need* to be there." She hadn't come this far to abandon the project now, and something within in her compelled her to go down to the wreck site again. It was almost as if she'd left something important there, though she hadn't a clue what that might be.

Adam looked at her a long moment, so long that the others began to shift uncomfortably in their chairs. Sandra refused to even blink. If he wanted a fight, she'd give him one, but she wasn't about to let him dictate what she could and could not do. "All right," he said finally. "As long as you don't exceed your normal diving time."

"What's the best way to get everything to the surface?" Charlie asked.

"We can pack things into crates at the site, then lift

them onto the *Caspian* with a hoist," Roger said. "It will mean maneuvering the ship practically on top of the wreck, but I'm sure they can do it safely."

"I want everything numbered and labeled," Adam said. "Matched with an inventory including written descriptions, photographs and drawings."

Brent nodded. "This is what I've been waiting for the entire trip."

"Every individual coin?" Merrick asked. "That will take forever."

"Not with all of us working, it won't," Adam said.

"A complete inventory is important not only for a historical record, but for when the treasure goes to auction," Tessa said.

"That's right," Adam agreed. "You don't want anything lost in transit, and you want every sale accounted for."

Merrick relaxed. "I see." He nodded. "Good job," he added grudgingly.

"Charlie, you and Tessa and Merrick can go down now and start photographing," Adam said.

They were on their feet before he'd finished speaking. "Merrick!" Adam called.

The financier stopped. "Yes?"

"Don't get any ideas about taking any souvenirs."

Roger rose from his chair. "I'll get to work on the hoist."

"I'll come up with a numbering and labeling system on the computer for classifying everything." Brent grabbed his crutch and rose also.

When they were alone in the room, Adam looked at Sandra. Before he could say anything, she stood also. "I'll head back to my yacht now," she said. "You were right. I should take it easy. At least the rest of the day."

She hurried from the room without saying anything

more. What was there to talk about when she didn't know what was happening to her? As she'd watched herself on camera, an idea had begun to form in her mind—an idea so outrageous it made her believe she might truly be going crazy. She needed to get away by herself for a few hours and try to sort this out. Maybe by the time she saw Adam again, she'd know what to say to him. And whether or not the two of them had any sort of future together.

14

ADAM HEFTED A SILVER BAR retrieved from the shipwreck and examined it for identifying marks. A diagonal slash cut across one corner of the heavy bar, which was also branded with the letter *C*. He recorded these on the spreadsheet opened on his laptop and returned the bar to the water tank in which it had been resting. This was bar number twenty of those they'd retrieved from the wreck so far. Nearby, Brent sketched the pattern on a porcelain plate they'd retrieved that morning.

Since locating the treasure yesterday, they'd recovered perhaps one-tenth of the most valuable items. Fragile pieces had to be brought up one piece at a time, while other items, such as the silver bars, were too heavy to be retrieved in large quantities. He knew Merrick chafed at the slow progress, but the billionaire was smart enough to keep quiet.

Not that his impatience wasn't obvious; right now he paced the other end of the room, stopping from time to time to watch the others work. "What are you doing now?" he asked Tessa as she arranged a handful of blackened gold coins in a metal basket inside of one of the water tanks.

"I'm going to run an electrical charge through the basket and that will help remove some of the tarnish from these coins," she explained.

"If you bother her anymore while she's trying to work,

she might decide to run that electrical current through you," Adam said.

Merrick turned away from Tessa and walked across the room to stand beside Adam. He studied the twenty-first silver bar Adam was examining. "Congratulations," Merrick said abruptly. "I really had my doubts at times, but you've really done it. You've found the *Eve*."

"We've found a ship with a lot of treasure," Brent said, looking up from his drawing. "But have we found any proof that this really is the *Eve?*"

Both men looked at Adam expectantly. He shook his head. "I'm sure the proof is there, but we haven't found it yet." The missing proof stole much of the joy of the find from Adam. As much as he appreciated the prospect of wealth from the sale of the treasure, his real purpose in launching this expedition had been to locate the infamous pirate ship, to link his name forever with that of the *Eve,* and with history.

"I don't see how it matters that much," Merrick said. "We've found treasure. It dates from the appropriate period, so what does it matter if it came from the *Eve* or from one of the ships Passionata attacked?"

"Provenance can enhance the value of the objects," Brent pointed out. "Both their historic worth and their monetary value."

"People don't just want a piece of pottery or a coin because it's old." Charlie set a tank containing the enameled box and two jeweled cups in the middle of the table. "They want something because it had ties to an infamous pirate. They want to believe their hands are touching something *she* once touched." He took a seat on the opposite end of the table, as far from Brent as possible. Ever since Sandra and Tessa had stranded him and Merrick on that atoll, he'd lost some of his bravado and kept his distance from his fellow interns.

Judging from the heated looks they exchanged when they thought no one was looking, Adam suspected Brent and Tessa were involved, though they continued to behave professionally on the job.

Merrick pulled out a chair and sat next to Adam. "What sort of thing would prove this wreck is the *Eve?*" he asked.

"It could be anything," Adam said. "A cannon with an inscription, or a ship's bell engraved with the ship's name. Even a personal artifact identifiable as belonging to Passionata would do."

"It's like building a criminal case based on circumstantial evidence," Brent said. He lifted the enameled box from the water tank and set it on a turntable in front of him, then turned to a fresh sheet in his sketch book, while Charlie checked the camera. While the camera recorded the exact image, drawings could fill in missing designs in the enamel or missing parts of the chest, and show cut-away views. Drawings supplied a view of how the object would have looked before it had spent three hundred years submerged in the ocean.

"It's a beautiful box." Tessa joined them around that table, coming to stand behind Brent. "It's too bad it didn't contain jewelry. Then we could have looked for photographs of Passionata wearing the pieces. That would link her to the box and thus to the ship."

"I still can't believe Sandra found it all by itself in that one grid," Charlie said. "I'd have never thought to look there myself."

"We would have located it eventually," Brent said. He turned the enameled chest over and scrutinized the underside with a jeweler's loup.

"What are you doing?" Merrick asked.

"I'm looking for a maker's mark," he said. "That could tell us when this was made, and where." He slipped off the loup and shook his head. "Nothing. I was hoping I might find initials or a name engraved there, too."

"You mean, like, Passionata?" Merrick asked.

"Or J.H.," Tessa said. "Her real name was Jane Hallowell."

"When we have time to research it more we might find out where it's from and what period," Charlie said. "It looks as if it might be a one-of-a-kind object."

"Has anyone talked to Sandra this morning?" Tessa asked. "Jonas was filming by himself at the wreck site."

She addressed her remarks to Adam and he shifted in his chair. He'd been meaning to visit Sandra, to make sure she was recovered from her fainting spell of yesterday, but he'd been so caught up in retrieving and cataloging the treasure he hadn't gotten around to it.

"I'm sure she's fine," he said, as much to reassure himself as the others. He shoved back from the table and stood. "I need to discuss the filming with her, anyway. Charlie, Brent, you finish up here."

They nodded. "Tell Sandra I hope she's feeling better," Tessa said.

"I'll do that." Then he left the room before anyone could make any comments, though he was aware of Merrick staring after him.

The steward, Rodrigo, welcomed Adam aboard the yacht. "Ms. Newman is expecting you in her cabin," he said, his expression inscrutable.

Adam thought this was a polite fiction considering he hadn't spoken to Sandra since yesterday morning. Guilt made him hurry down the passage to her cabin, where he hesitated before knocking. "Sandra, it's me, Adam."

The door opened and she stood before him, dressed in a long, red silk gown and matching robe, looking like the glamorous star of a 1940s movie, her dark hair tumbling around her shoulders. The look she gave him was positively smoldering, and desire hit him sharp and fierce. He thought of himself as a man guided by his intellect and not his instincts, but when he was with Sandra, he felt this desire that went beyond conscious thought to elemental need.

"I had a feeling you'd stop by soon," she said, holding the door open wider and motioning for him to come in."

"I meant to check up on you yesterday," he said. "Working with the treasure took more time than I anticipated."

"That's all right," she said, her voice soft and low. Seductive. "I knew you'd come today."

The way she said this, with such certainty, made the hair on the back of his neck stand up. "How did you know?" he asked.

"You and I have a connection now." She walked over to him and rested both palms flat on his chest. His skin felt hot where she touched him. "In fact, I think the two of us getting together here, on Passionata's Island, was inevitable."

Before he could think of an answer to this strange statement, her lips covered his and he was lost in her kiss. He closed his eyes and pulled her to him, the feel of her body shaped to his, calling forth responses that were as automatic as breathing, as intense as the insistent beat of his heart.

The red silk slipped beneath his fingers as he pushed the robe from her shoulders, then bunched the fabric of the gown at her hip. She was naked beneath the silk, and the knowledge made him grow harder.

She arched against him, and he bent to take one breast in his mouth, his tongue sliding the fabric back and forth across the sensitive tip. She thrust hard against him, pressing against his erection with an uninhibited wantonness that increased his eagerness for her. He suckled harder, then moved to the other breast, all the while holding her tightly against him. "See what you've done to me?" she whispered in his ear. "I can't get enough of you."

And he would never get enough of her. She was like the sunrise over the waves, always beautiful, yet different every day. He couldn't imagine ever tiring of her as he had other women he'd known; the knowledge was both exhilarating and terrifying.

They undressed each other, hands and mouths exploring, each knowing where to touch the other to elicit the greatest response. She cupped his balls in her hand, massaging gently as she nipped at his chest, then trailing her nails the length of his back, awakening every nerve to an awareness of her.

He laid her on the bed and parted her thighs, staring at her sex. She'd shaved herself bare, and the shock and eroticism of the gesture left him speechless. "It's what you've always wanted, isn't it?" she asked, grinning.

He cleared his throat. That *was* a particular fantasy of his, but one he'd never shared with her. Had she guessed, or was it merely a common fantasy, shared by many men— men she'd known before? "I know you, Adam," she said, as if to reassure him. "I know you better than I ever realized before. And you know me."

He *did* know her body, as well as any man could know a woman. In the few weeks they'd been together she'd become as familiar to him as a part of himself. He knew if he trailed his fingers across her stomach, she was ticklish, but that the same light touch along the inside of her thighs soon had her panting for him. She loved for him to kiss and caress her breasts, but had no patience for him touching her backside.

She arched to him now, and he accepted the silent invitation and traced his tongue along the folds and hollows of her sex, tickling and teasing, fast, then slow; softly, then with insistent pressure. She buried her fingers in his hair, urging him on with throaty moans and whispered pleas. Her active, passionate response to his every movement made him all the more determined to delight her.

And delight her he did, to judge by her cries as she came, thrusting hard against his mouth, then reaching for him, pulling him up to her. His mouth covered hers, muffling her cries as he slid into her. She tightened around him, squeezing his cock until a groan escaped him. "Did I hurt you?" she asked, eyes opened wide.

"No." He put his hand on her hip and thrust deeply into her. "Never."

Smiling, she rocked beneath him, eyes locked to his, as if she could never get enough of looking at him. He fought the urge to close his eyes and kept his gaze steady on her, letting her see what loving her was doing to him, making him so vulnerable and needy, and at the same time stronger and more powerful than he had ever been.

She wrapped her legs around his hips and tilted her pelvis to accept him more fully, her movements perfectly matched to his, as if they'd been making love for a lifetime. When she'd spoken of a connection between them, is this what she'd meant?

Then he forgot the question as his climax overtook him, rolling over him in waves, deep and satisfying.

For a long while afterward they lay in each other's arms, her hands playing lightly over his shoulder and back, caressing and stroking, not so much in a gesture of comfort as for the sheer pleasure of touching him.

Finally he slid from her, and she left the bed and disappeared into the bathroom. She returned after a few minutes and joined him under the covers. "I hope this means you've recovered from whatever was wrong yesterday," he said, as she settled with her head resting in the hollow of his shoulder.

"Yes, today I'm feeling much better."

"What happened?" he asked. "Was it another one of those strange spells, like before?"

She hesitated, then nodded. "Yes. I think so."

"You should see a doctor when we get back to the States," he said. What if this was a symptom of a brain tumor, or something equally as dire? The thought made him cold, and he put his arm around her protectively, as if he could somehow keep her from danger.

"Don't you mean a psychiatrist?"

The hard edge in her voice unsettled him. He stroked her shoulder. "I don't think you're crazy," he said. "But you're obviously not yourself."

She stiffened but didn't move away. "Were you able to bring much of the treasure to the surface yet?" she asked.

"Some. It's slow going, documenting everything, then packing the fragile items to keep them from being damaged on the way up from the bottom. Then we have to treat them carefully once they're up here, decide how best to preserve them, and catalog each one."

"I want to film all of that," she said. "Viewers will be interested in a behind-the-scenes look at the treasure. We can use before and after shots."

The excitement in her voice ought to have been contagious, but he was unable to enjoy his find as long as questions about its source hung over him. "I still don't have any proof the wreck is really the *Eve*," he said.

"It's the *Eve*," she said.

"How do you know?"

She raised her head and looked at him, her hair falling like a dark curtain around them, shutting out the rest of the world. Shutting out doubt. "I know. The same way I knew that jewel chest would be in that one grid."

"How *did* you know about the chest?" he asked. "And don't say it was women's intuition. There had to be a reason you were so insistent we look in that particular place."

Worry etched fine lines at the corners of her eyes. "Promise you won't think I'm crazy."

"I promise."

She inhaled deeply, and pressed her lips together for a moment before she said, "I think all these things that are happening to me—the dizzy spells and hallucinations and my knowing about the chest—all of them have something to do with Passionata."

He tried to make sense of this but couldn't. "I don't understand."

She sat up, drawing her knees to her chest and gathering the sheets around her. "Do you remember the night you came to my cabin? I was fine, then all of a sudden, I was someone else. I mean, it was as if someone else had taken over my body."

"You *were* acting strange," he said, remembering how she had clung to him, and how hard it had been to leave her.

"It was as if I was in a dream, but so realistic—more vivid than any dream I've ever had. This man whose name keeps coming up, Frederick, was making love to me. But he looked like you."

He grinned. "I knew you had the hots for me."

"Yes. No. Not *you*. This Frederick guy. But it wasn't really *me* lusting after him. It was Passionata."

"It was a dream," he said.

"What about the next time, when I visited the tower?

Passionata's old headquarters. Standing on the top floor I saw furnishings that weren't there. I felt tapestries on the wall. I knew everything in that room, as if it was my own. Everything that had belonged to Passionata. And then downstairs, with you. I had the same feeling as before, of not having control over my own body. And you were making love to me, but it wasn't you at all. It was Frederick."

The wild look in her eyes worried him. He sat and took her by the shoulders. "That was me making love to you," he said. "Just as it was me right now."

She shook her head, her face contorted with misery. "Do you remember when you showed me the jeweled dagger?"

He nodded. "You had another one of your spells." What else to call her strange behavior that day?

"I recognized the dagger," she said. "I knew it was mine. Not mine, but Passionata's. It was as if, for a moment there, I *was* Passionata. It was the same feeling I'd had in the tower, and again when you and I were making love."

"So when you and I have sex, you're not you? You're caught up in some fantasy or hallucination that you're Passionata."

"No! Not every time. And even in those times, I know it's you." She hugged her arms around her knees and rocked back and forth. "It's so hard to explain. I know you're you and I'm me and we're having an amazing time together. But it's also as if I'm Passionata and you're Frederick. I know things about you I couldn't know unless we'd been together for a long time before. And I feel things for you it would be impossible to feel for a man I'd only known a few weeks."

"What kind of things?" he asked, holding his breath as he waited for her answer.

Her eyes met his, and the desperation he saw there

shook him. "That I love you, and I need you," she said, her voice ragged with tears.

Her words shook him. Yes, he had feelings for her, too—but *love?* Love involved commitment, expectations, responsibility. He swallowed hard.

She stared at him, her expression hardening. "What's wrong?" she asked. "Why are you so quiet?"

"I'm trying to understand this," he said. "But I need your help. Are you saying Passionata is—what? Possessing you?"

"Not…possessing, exactly. But maybe…maybe I *was* Passionata, in another life."

"Reincarnation?"

She nodded, still looking miserable. "I know it's wild, but it's the only explanation I can think of. I was Passionata and now that I'm on the island, I'm remembering that part of my past."

"Then who is Frederick?"

"I think he's the pirate who betrayed her. Her first love, the man she never really got over."

"Nothing in her book or the other documents about her mention anyone named Frederick," he said.

"I know. But that was his name. I know it, the way I knew the enameled chest would be there in that grid."

He studied her, wanting to believe her, but unsure he could ever accept such a wild explanation. Reincarnation? Possession? Each idea seemed equally bizarre.

And yet…Sandra had known about the chest. And she had reacted strangely to the tower and the dagger. Something not entirely logical was going on here.

"Do you believe me?" she asked.

"I believe something is happening to you," he said. "And it does seem to be connected to Passionata and the shipwreck in some way. I've never been one to ignore hunches.

But if you're asking if I believe that you and I were lovers in another lifetime…" He shook his head. "I don't know if I can go that far."

"If I found some proof that the wreck is that of the *Eve*, would you believe me then?" she asked.

"I don't know," he admitted. "I don't know if I'm capable of going that far." She'd already asked him to go further than he'd ever gone with a woman, into the murky depths known as love. He didn't know if he could bring himself to dive that deep. "Why don't we wait and see what happens?" he said.

"You think I'm crazy, don't you?" she said, pulling away from him.

"No, I don't. But you've been working hard. And you're a strong, independent woman. It's no surprise you'd identify strongly with Passionata. It's not even surprising you'd dream about her. But I don't think that's proof you *were* her. Or are her." The more he talked, the more logical his explanation sounded. He felt in control of the situation again, and relieved to be standing once more on firm ground.

"You don't believe me," she said again, her voice flat. "Why did I expect you to behave differently than any other *man?* I'm just the silly little woman who needs humoring. I *hate* being humored." She stood, dragging most of the bed covers with her. "You'd better go."

"Sandra, there's no need to be angry with me," he said.

"Of course not. But I'm just a crazy, illogical *woman.* And I'm angry." She glared at him, the heat of her gaze making him flinch. "Get out."

He started to argue, then gathered his clothes and left the room, dressing in the sitting room before letting himself out of the cabin. Maybe Sandra was crazy. Or at least unstable. Just as well he was getting out of the relationship now. The thoughts did nothing to ease the ache in his heart. Maybe when he was farther away from her bed, further removed from the intense emotion of the past hour, he'd be truly grateful to have escaped a trap that might have injured him more if they'd tried to take this fantasy back to the States.

Maybe time would ease the pain he felt now, but he had his doubts. Whatever else he could say about Sandra, she'd touched a part of him he'd never allowed anyone to touch before. Having known her, he'd never be the same again. And every other woman he met would always lack something essential. He cursed her for that as much as for anything else she'd given him.

15

SANDRA SLUMPED onto the end of the bed, blankets wrapped around her as if she could somehow ward off the chill that had washed over her at the sound of the door slamming behind Adam. As fantastic as she knew her reincarnation theory had been, it hurt that he hadn't believed her. Would *she* have believed him if their roles were reversed? She wanted to think she would, that the feelings of her heart would have overruled the logic of her brain, but how could she really know?

She stood, determined to shake off the depression that threatened to crush her. Everything in her life hadn't fallen apart. The documentary was coming together well. Jonas had gotten great footage of the treasure they'd found, and everyone on the crew had given her great interviews that would help tell the story of the expedition. The network, and more important, the viewers, would love this show. Her ratings would rise and she'd be secure in her job, even if she had lost Adam. She fingered the golden globe her grandmother gave her. "I'm having those adventures, Grandma," she whispered. "Just not the one I want most." She'd never risked a long-term relationship with a man before, and it looked as if her best chance for that had passed her by.

Restless, she picked up her copy of *Confessions of a*

Pirate Queen and flipped through it. What would Passionata do in her situation? The pirate queen had had her heart broken and had found the strength to go on. Could her experience offer any guidance to Sandra?

She turned to the front of the book, looking for Passionata's account of her lover's betrayal, and began to read:

For two weeks I stole away several times a week to meet my lover. We strolled fashionable London streets, and he bought me expensive baubles from fine shops. Few of my acquaintances knew him, and I kept my face veiled to avoid being recognized. Other times, late at night, we would rendezvous at my father's office. There was a sameness to our encounters that approached ritual. He always began by studying the charts on the office walls, and sometimes browsed the stacks of papers on the desk— papers we had to move aside to make room for our activities.

Always the undressing. Always the slow build of sensation toward the fabulous end that left me feeling more magical and powerful than I had ever imagined—and yet left me wanting more.

We met this way for over a fortnight, and if no outer change was evident to others, a profound inner change was taking place. I thought of little else but my pirate and how I might please him. I counted the hours to our next assignation, and many days when I was not with him were spent remembering the last time I had been with him, and imagining the next time.

I had not seen him in two days when a great alarm woke our whole household very early on a Friday morning. As I pulled on a dressing gown and squinted out at the pale dawn, a servant rushed into the room. "You must go to your father, immediately," she said, and took hold of my hand and dragged me after her.

My father was downstairs in his study, two grim-looking men I recognized as business acquaintances with him. When I entered the room, they regarded me with cold eyes, while my father stared as if he did not recognize me.

His appearance—hair uncombed and uncovered by his usual wig, face the color of ashes, eyes watery and unfocused—alarmed me greatly. I rushed to his side and bade him sit down. "Father, what is wrong?" I cried, growing more anguished by the moment.

"All gone," he moaned. "Everything is gone."

I stared up at the other two men. "What is he talking about?" I asked. "What is all gone?"

"We received word this morning," the younger of the two said. "In separate raids over the past three days, five of your father's ships have been attacked and sunk."

"Attacked?" The word refused to register. "Who would do such a thing?"

The two men exchanged glances and worried looks.

"Tell me!" I demanded. "I must know."

"It is the work of pirates," the older man said.

My blood froze, and I struggled to remain standing, still supporting my father. "Pirates?" my voice had a strained, high-pitched quality.

"Yes." Then he uttered the name I dreaded to hear. That of my lover. My pirate. He had attacked the man I loved second only to him, destroying my father by destroying his world.

The next days were a blur of meetings and

visitors—lawyers, investors and creditors seques-
tered themselves with my father in his office for
hours, and each time he emerged grayer and more
drawn than before.

I sent word by the usual messengers for my pirate
to meet me, to no avail. More reports of damages
came in and I felt my heart grow harder with each
one; five ships damaged beyond repair. All cargo
lost. Most of the crew perished.

At the end of a week my father was left with one
ship that was his alone. Men took away the carriage
and horses. Others took the parlor and dining furni-
ture. A third set of men came to measure draperies and
to ask how soon the building would be available to let.

I did my best to help my father and to comfort
him, all the while seething at my former lover, who
had so cruelly taken me in and used me. Whatever
feelings I had imagined myself to have for him
burned to ash in a white-hot rage.

By the end of the second week, all was quiet once
more. Father and I sat in the nearly empty town
house, silence making the rooms seem twice as big,
the distance between the two of us uncrossable.

"We are ruined," my father announced that night,
in the voice of the grave.

"Is it so bad at that?" I asked. "You still have one
ship left."

"No one will trust a cargo to a man so cursed as
I," he said. "We have lost our berth in port, lost our
office and will soon lose the house, as well. I have
no savings. No dowry for you."

"What will we do?" I asked.

He shook his head but said nothing.

I lay awake half the night, contemplating a future as a ladies' companion or governess, cursing the pirate who had stolen so much from me. My only comfort was that he had not taken more. He had not stolen my father or my health, or my ability to find a way out of this dilemma.

Long past midnight I heard the gunshot. A single report from the direction of my father's room. I lay in bed for a long time, knowing what this meant— what my father's despair had pushed him to.

When the maid came I rose and dressed and ordered tea. I set out to make the arrangements to bury my father with the dignity he deserved. The servants and family friends marveled at my strength, at the fact that I shed not one visible tear throughout this ordeal.

They did not realize I had no room left in my heart for sorrow—hate had filled every nook and cranny of my soul.

On a rainy Monday I stood in the graveyard and tossed dirt and roses onto my father's coffin. I watched as it was lowered into the ground and covered with soil, heard the murmured condolences of the other mourners, then returned in a hired carriage to the home that would be mine for very little longer. I sat in the parlor for a long while, staring at the fire.

I did not cry; I planned. And in the morning I dressed in my sturdiest gown, packed a trunk with other sturdy gowns and undergarments, and set out for the wharf.

Not pausing to consider the recklessness of my folly, I walked into the first seaman's bar I saw. I took part of the cash I had received from a small insurance settlement and laid it on the bar. "I am looking to hire a crew," I said.

"You have a ship?" the bartender asked.

"Yes. The *Intrepid.* She is anchored in the harbor." It was all I had left to me, and I was determined it should be the means of my salvation.

He nodded to a table in the corner of the room, where a half-dozen men gathered around a dice game. I repeated my offer to them.

"Where are you headed?" asked a grizzled seaman with only one eye.

"Tortuga," I said. The island of pirates. Where I hoped to find the man who had stolen everything from me. When I saw him, I intended to shoot him through the heart and cut off his balls.

The man I had loved, to whom I had given my all, had never loved me. He had used me, to learn the secrets of my father's business—the routes of my father's ships and their cargos. He had struck like a cobra, taking all, destroying my father.

Destroying me.

Or so he thought. But I would not be destroyed. Not when the creditors came to auction the house and all our belongings. Not when my father took his own life by shooting himself with a pistol. I died, too, then. Jane Hallowell died.

But Passionata was born.

ADAM BROKE THROUGH the surface of the ocean, water streaming from his hair and mask, and handed the net bag containing a pair of gold cups to Roger in the dive boat. Merrick and Charlie surfaced nearby. "There are only a couple more cups down there," Adam said as Roger helped the men into the boat. "We're making good progress."

"Too bad there isn't more to bring up," Roger said. "I still think we're missing something."

Before Adam could answer, Roger fired up the boat motor and headed toward the *Caspian*. Adam frowned at his back. Everyone had clamored for treasure and he'd found it, but of course, it was never enough. They always wanted more.

He wanted more. The more he studied the objects they'd found, the more he believed Roger was right: part of the ship was missing. If he found that part and the treasure it contained, would he also find the proof he needed that this wreck was really the *Eve?* He wanted that more than almost anything.

And he wanted Sandra. Crazy or sane, he wanted her, but he didn't know how to ask her to forgive him for the harsh words he'd said at their last meeting. Or even if he should. Maybe it was just as well they'd ended things now, before the good times of the summer turned into bad times in their everyday lives.

Even this argument did nothing to ease the pain of losing her. He'd thrown himself into his work, his usual approach to dealing with problems. But he could only dive so many minutes each day, and in the workroom it was too easy to let his mind wander.

They'd moved the entire operation back to the boat, and this added to his restlessness. As much as he enjoyed sailing, stuck on a motionless craft in the middle of the water for twenty-three hours a day left him restless. He sometimes took walks on the beach but that made him think of Sandra, too.

Not that he didn't see her. She'd been near him all day, filming the salvage expedition. She didn't look at him or speak to him, and he had to bite his tongue and force himself to look away from her.

On board the ship, the crew changed clothes and met again in the galley. They were eating lunch when Roger burst into the room with all the force of a gale. "Weather report just came in," he said, slapping down a computer printout in the middle of the table. "We've got another tropical storm headed this way, expected to reach hurricane force by tomorrow."

A collective groan rose from the group. A storm meant delays they could ill afford. "We'll try to bring up twice as much tomorrow," Adam said. "We can spend the time during the storm cataloging the objects."

"We shouldn't try to wait this one out here," Roger said. "It's too big and moving too fast."

Adam frowned. "When is it predicted to reach us?" he asked.

"Day after tomorrow. We need to get all the equipment in and head for Jamaica before it gets here."

"Can't we ride it out?" Merrick asked. "The way we did the last one?"

"A hurricane isn't the same as a tropical storm," Roger said. "And this one is shaping up to be a big one. You can stay here if you like, but I've already talked to the captain and he's leaving tomorrow afternoon, whether you like it or not."

As much as Adam wanted to continue the salvage operation, he wouldn't risk his crew or equipment. "We'd better go," he said. "We can come back later."

"The summer's almost over," Brent said, his expression glum.

"We can make another expedition next summer," Adam said. "We've got enough artifacts to show now that it shouldn't be hard to get the funding for a second trip. We can search for the missing stern of the ship then."

"So we leave everything down there until then?" Merrick asked. "What's to keep someone else from coming along and robbing us?"

"Nothing," Adam said. "Except it wouldn't be worth it for them, since we should be able to retrieve the most valuable objects before we leave."

"All but whatever's in that missing section of the ship," Roger said.

"If there is a missing section," Adam said. "And if we don't know where it is, no one else does, either." He shook his head. "I'm not happy about leaving, but I don't see that we have a choice."

Merrick studied him a long moment. "I want to come back next year," he said. "I'll put up the money again."

The offer surprised Adam. After the grief they'd given him, he'd expected Merrick to jump at the chance to be rid of them. Instead he'd continued to work alongside them, until he now seemed like a real member of the team. "Thank you," Adam said. "I'd be happy to have you as part of the team."

"Yeah," Merrick said gruffly. "It's been good being a part of this," he said. "And it's a great deal more interesting than spending the summer at the yacht club."

"I wouldn't know," Adam said. But he was grinning. Merrick wasn't such a bad guy, now that he'd stopped pursuing Sandra and slacked off on trying to boss everyone around.

They had the promise of next year, anyway. Maybe he could persuade Sandra to return with them, to make a follow-up documentary. Alone on the island again, who knew? They might find a way to patch things up between them, or at least indulge in another summer of fantasy. She'd already given him a summer he'd never forget, but he wasn't ready for it to end.

THAT NIGHT Sandra dreamed she was diving alone, the water dark and cool around her. She moved with the ease only found in dreams, as if floating through air, graceful and weightless. She swam through a school of clown fish, who flowed around her like orange and white confetti, and passed over the wreck site.

Except that the ship below her was not decayed and disintegrating, but as perfect as if it had just been set down on the ocean floor, white sails rippling in the current, brass cannons polished and gleaming, rigging taut and square.

Only when she drew nearer did Sandra see that the back third of the ship was missing, as if ripped away by a giant. Below the jagged boards of the deck she could see the hammocks where the crew slept, and a hold neatly stacked with trunks, barrels and crates.

She wanted to stop and explore further, but was compelled to move on, leaving the ship behind. She moved without effort and soon found herself over the stern of the ship. Like the rest of the vessel, this sat pristine and undisturbed on the ocean floor, the teak railing gleaming, the aft sails fully rigged and billowing in the current. Sandra alighted on the deck, and found she was dressed, not in scuba gear, but in boots, breeches and a long-tailed coat. She strode across the deck, her steps soundless, past the mast to a barrel near the railing. Reaching down, she pulled from behind the barrel a gleaming cutlass. She held the blade up, turning it this way and that, admiring the way the light glinted off the steel, and reflected in the ruby eyes of the bronze serpent coiled around the hilt. Then she sheathed the weapon at her side and walked to the broken edge of the deck, and stepped off into nothingness….

She woke with a start and sat up in bed, staring into the darkness around her. As her heartbeat slowed and her breathing began to return to normal, she tried to make sense of the dream. The whole point of her underwater journey had seemed to be to retrieve the sword. But why?

The ruby-eyed serpent on the hilt of the weapon had seemed so familiar. Was it because the sword had belonged to Passionata? The renewed quickening of her heart told her she'd hit upon the solution. If Adam had this sword, he'd have the proof he needed that the wreck he'd discovered was the *Eve*.

Had Passionata sent the dream to reveal the hiding place of the sword? If so, did that mean the curse was a myth, that she didn't mind that Adam—Frederick—had uncovered her treasure?

Or was she happy that through Sandra she was being given a second chance to create a happier ending with her lover.

Hah! A lover who clearly thought Sandra was unstable, and not the sort of woman a respectable university professor ought to associate with. She'd never pegged Adam for a snob, but what else was she supposed to think, considering how he'd avoided speaking or even looking at her the past few days?

Maybe fate had determined that they were two souls, in whatever bodies, who could never be together.

The argument struck her as a cop-out. Why did fate get to decide this? She and Adam were both intelligent adults. If they wanted to be together, why couldn't they find a way to work this out?

Finding the sword might be a good place to start. If nothing else, she could prove to him—and to herself—that she wasn't crazy, and that he'd been wrong to underestimate her.

16

"ONE MORE DIVE today and we should have all the most-valuable items up," Adam said, as he pulled himself into the dive boat and stripped off his mask.

"You can't go back down again," Roger said, handing him a towel. "You're already over your diving time."

"It's the last day." He ran the towel over his face and hair. "I promise I'll take it easy coming back up."

"That's what you said yesterday." Roger wore a perpetual scowl, so it was difficult to tell if he was any more upset than usual. "We're a long way from a decompression chamber out here. No treasure is worth dying for."

The loud roar of an approaching boat motor cut off Adam's answer. They looked up and saw Sam steering a Zodiac toward them. Brent rode with him. Sam pulled alongside them and cut the engine. "Everybody needs to get back to the ship now," he said.

Just then, Merrick and Charlie surfaced. "What's up?" Charlie called.

"An updated weather report just came in," Sam said. "Larry's a category-three storm, moving faster than predicted and gaining strength. It could be a category five by tomorrow. We have to get out of here, pronto."

Adam looked at Roger. "I thought you said it wasn't supposed to be here until tomorrow night."

"Since when have you known a weather forecaster to be one-hundred-percent accurate?" Sam asked. "Anyway, the captain says we've got half an hour to haul in our gear, then he's pulling up anchor and heading for safer waters."

Adam wanted to argue, but realized it would do no good. "You heard what he said," he told the others. "We'd better get busy."

They were all in the boats, removing their diving gear when Brent spoke up. "Where's Tessa?" he asked.

Adam looked around, surprised the intern wasn't with them. "Wasn't she with you, Charlie?" he asked.

Charlie shook his head. "Sandra said she needed her help with something. The two of them headed off together—I thought to the other side of the wreck."

"Where's Sandra?" Adam asked. As usual, she'd joined them this morning with her camera, but had entered the water before he'd had a chance to speak with her. He'd grown used to her working in the background, though come to think of it, he hadn't seen her in a while. "Has anyone seen Sandra?"

No one had. His stomach churned. He'd started out the day determined to find the opportunity to talk with her. When she'd successfully avoided him this morning, he'd told himself he'd go to her yacht later. He wouldn't let her leave angry at him. She might not want him as her lover, but he valued her friendship.

"Maybe she went back to her yacht already," Merrick said.

"Did you see her, Roger?" Adam asked.

Roger shook his head. "Rodrigo took her Zodiac back to her yacht right after he dropped her off this morning. He said she'd catch a ride back to the *Caspian* with us."

Adam reached for a new set of diving tanks. "I'm going down to look for her."

"But your time—"

He silenced Roger's protest with a glare. "I'll go with you," Charlie said, and zipped up his wet suit once more.

"No." Adam connected his regulator and started a safety check. "You're over your dive time."

"Let me come," Brent said. "I haven't dived for a week."

"What about your knee?" Adam asked.

He shrugged. "It'll be fine in the water."

"All right." He needed someone down there with him, and even with a bum knee, Brent was at less risk than any of the others. "Hurry and suit up."

While the others helped Brent into diving gear, Adam tried to imagine where the women might be. Were they injured, unnoticed by the others in the hurry to recover as many artifacts as possible in the time left to them? Had they wandered away and been attacked by a shark? Or had they returned to Sandra's yacht already, and all his worry was for nothing?

"Sam, go over to Sandra's yacht and see if she and Tessa are there," he said. And if she was, he'd personally go over there and kiss her—then read her the riot act for frightening him this way.

SANDRA SWAM near the ocean bottom much as she had swum in her dream, though this time she was not alone. Worried she might suffer another of the odd spells that had plagued her, she'd pulled Tessa aside and persuaded her to accompany her. When they were away from the others, she'd written a cryptic explanation on her slate—that she'd seen something she wanted to investigate. She had to find out if her dream image was real—if the stern of the ship was where the dream had shown her it would be, and if Passionata's cutlass was there.

Tessa, swimming alongside her, kept giving her curious looks, but continued to follow Sandra's lead as they swam farther and farther from the wreck and the others. The back of Sandra's neck began to tingle, and her heart beat faster. They were getting close, she was sure of it.

Suddenly, a wall of coral rose up in front of them. It was too small to be a reef. Was it a new reef forming, or an older section separated from the main reef by a storm or other phenomena?

Tessa grabbed Sandra's wrist and pointed. Peering closer, Sandra made out a large fan shape made of rusting iron. As her eyes registered the shape, her brain supplied an identification: this was a ship's rudder.

Shaking with excitement, she swam up and over the reef. The two women stared down on what was clearly the remains of a ship. Was it the missing portion of the *Eve,* broken off and settled here, about a quarter of a mile from the main body of the ship?

Tessa pumped her fist, then gave Sandra an awkward hug. Sandra studied the wreckage, trying to recall the exact location of the sword in her dream. Taking out her camera, she turned it on and handed it to Tessa, indicating the young woman should film everything around them. Then Sandra swam down to the debris field. Tessa grabbed her ankle, trying to hold her back, but Sandra shook her off. Now that she'd found the rest of the ship, she wasn't leaving without that sword.

At first she saw nothing but debris and sea life. A colony of black and purple anemones covered an iron stanchion that had once held a mast, and a small octopus flowed over a collapsing barrel. In her dream, she—Passionata—had removed the sword from behind a barrel. At first, Sandra saw nothing resembling a sword, then, to the left of the octopus, she caught a glimpse of red. Diving closer, she saw a single ruby eye staring at her from a coiled bronze serpent.

The tip of the weapon was sheared off, the blade dull with rust and one of the serpent's ruby eyes was missing. But this was the sword—Passionata's blade. As Sandra's hand closed around the hilt she felt energy surge through her, and for one brief second she was standing on the deck of the *Eve,* both ship and sword whole and gleaming. A strong sea breeze blew back her hair and the tails of her long coat, but she was immovable. She was the pirate queen, strong and invincible.

Then Tessa touched her arm and Sandra was back to herself. Tessa stared at the cutlass and Sandra handed it to her. The younger woman traced a finger over the serpent's eyes, and then over the jagged break in the blade. She handed it back to Sandra and indicated they should return to the others.

Sandra nodded. She couldn't wait to show this to Adam. Here was the proof he needed that he had indeed found the *Eve.* It might not be enough to convince him of her connection to Passionata, but she hoped he would accept this as proof that she loved him, no matter what their future held. She had retrieved this for him as much as for herself.

They left the wreckage and swam back the way they'd come. At least, Sandra thought it was the way they'd come, until she realized nothing looked familiar. She glanced at Tessa and saw that the younger woman, too, looked confused. They stopped and faced each other, Sandra searching around them for some landmark around which to orient herself. But the ocean floor was as unfamiliar to her as a moonscape.

Tessa clutched at her arm, and mouthed the one word Sandra had tried to avoid thinking. *Lost.* The women were lost in the vast ocean. She hadn't told anyone where she was going. How long before they were missed and the others began to search? And how long after that before they were found? If they were ever found.

ADAM AND BRENT SEARCHED the wreck site over and over, but there was no sign of the women. Adam tried to tell himself that was good—if they were trapped or had been attacked, he would have seen some sign of them by now. They were probably on Sandra's yacht, having a drink and laughing about once again having made fools of the men in their lives.

He was still hopeful when they surfaced at the Zodiac once more, but that hope died when Sam met him at the side of the boat. "Rodrigo says he hasn't seen Sandra or Tessa since he dropped Sandra off this morning."

"We didn't see any sign of them below, either." Brent stripped off his mask and tossed it onto the deck, then pulled off his flippers, his shoulders slumped, his expression dejected.

Adam took off his own gear, weariness making his limbs feel leaden. He had no idea where to look next. It wasn't like looking for someone on land, where one could follow tracks.

"Where could they have gone?" Charlie asked.

"How the hell should I know?" Adam snapped. He ran his hand over his face and tried to think, but worry and panic crowded out all attempts at logical thought. What would he do if he lost Sandra? He squeezed his eyes shut against the idea.

"You were close to her, weren't you?" Brent said. "Did she mention wanting to explore some other part of the ocean? Had she seen something she wanted to check out?"

He shook his head, not wasting his breath denying he and Sandra had been close. What did it matter now anyway? "What made her take off like that?" he wondered aloud. She'd been smart enough not to go by herself, but all that meant now was that they were looking for two women instead of one. Had she had one of her spells? Had Passionata—or what she thought was Passionata—persuaded her to take off on some wild quest?

"I don't know how much longer we can stay out here," Roger said. "The captain of the *Caspian* is anxious to leave."

"I'm not leaving without Sandra and Tessa," Adam said.

"We can leave you with the Zodiac," Sam said. "And you've still got your yacht."

"Tell the captain if he tries to haul anchor, I'll break his arm." Adam felt almost calm as he spoke, but he meant the words. He felt capable of such violence right now.

If only they hadn't argued last time he and Sandra were together. Who was he to dismiss the idea of reincarnation any more than he would dismiss the idea of heaven or hell? He was a historian—what did he know about supernatural phenomena?

One thing Sandra had said had rung true—there was a connection between the two of them that he'd never experienced with another woman. He'd been powerfully attracted to her since their first meeting here last summer. He'd shied away from pursuing that attraction because he'd made a policy of avoiding complications when it came to relationships, and Sandra was one of the most complicated women he'd met. She was a larger-than-life character—bold and beautiful, much as he'd imagined Passionata herself had been.

He'd never have believed he shared any characteristics with the seventeenth-century pirate who'd loved her then betrayed her, yet when he was with her, he did feel bolder than usual, and was it so far-fetched to think his love of sailing and the sea had come from more than summers spent with his uncle?

If there was anything to her belief that they were meant to be together—that they were reenacting Passionata and Frederick's ill-fated romance—was it because this time things were supposed to work out differently? This time, were they supposed to stay together? If there was any of Frederick in him, couldn't he call upon that part of himself to help him face any complications loving Sandra might bring into his life?

He closed his eyes and tried to concentrate. If he and Sandra were somehow psychically connected, shouldn't he be able to sense where she was right now?

Sandra, where are you? I'm sorry I didn't believe you. I realize how much I need you.

Don't leave me alone again.

SANDRA AND TESSA SURFACED, bobbing in the waves. The seas were rougher than they had been. Was it because they were farther from shore or because the weather was changing?

"I don't see anything," Tessa said, arching her neck. Both women had pushed their masks on top of their heads and were trying to see over the waves. "Not the island or the ship or anything."

Sandra swallowed hard and tried to breathe evenly, to remain calm. Nothing out here looked familiar, but they couldn't be that far from the others, could they?

A large swell tossed them apart, and she struggled to swim back to Tessa. "I'm getting seasick, bobbing around like this," the younger woman said.

Panic must be an antidote to motion sickness, Sandra

thought. Her stomach was fine, though she couldn't say the same for her nerves. She felt at her side for the propylene bag in which she'd sheathed the cutlass. Its weight dragged at her, but she refused to leave it behind.

"What do we do now?" Tessa asked. Her eyes were wide, her voice strained.

Sandra checked her gauges. "I'm too low on air to dive again," she said. "We should wait here for rescue. The others will have missed us by now and they'll be looking." At least, she hoped they would.

"Let's activate our glow-tubes." Tessa held up the small chemical cylinder that, when broken, served as a marker and emergency light to make it easier for passing craft to see them in the water.

Sandra activated her tube, then tried to get comfortable in the rough seas. Taking a deep breath, she closed her eyes and sent a silent message to Adam. He hadn't believed her before, but even out here in the middle of the ocean she felt closer to him than she ever had to anyone else. His logical mind might not believe her words, but the bond between them went beyond words. His heart had to believe the emotions they shared, whether the man would admit it or not.

ADAM GUIDED THE ZODIAC out over the empty water while Brent, perched in the bow of the craft with a pair of binoculars, scanned the waves for some sign of the two women. When Adam had proposed heading out to search again, Roger had thought he was mad and had tried to restrain him.

In the end it was Merrick who took Adam's side. "Let him go," he said. "If he thinks he knows where they are, let him search."

Roger released his hold on Adam and stepped back. "If

you're going to do this, take my binoculars," he said, and retrieved a pair from a storage box and thrust them at Adam.

"I'm going with you," Brent said, already headed for the Zodiac.

"Good luck," Merrick said, and clapped him on the shoulder.

"Thanks. I figure we need it."

"Why do you think they're out here?" Brent shouted his question over the steady hum of the motor and the roar of the wind. "This is a long way from the wreck."

"I just have a feeling," he said. A feeling that was getting stronger each minute. They were on the right track, he knew it.

Brent turned to point the binoculars over the bow once more. "Look!" he shouted, and pointed to the east.

Adam throttled down the motor and strained to see in the direction Brent pointed. In a moment he made out the phosphorous glow of a chemical lighting tube.

"There's someone floating out there," Brent said. "Two someones! It has to be them."

Adam raced the boat toward the light. In between the swell of waves he kept his gaze fixed on the two floating figures. When they were close enough to make out faces, the women began to shout and wave.

He managed to hold the Zodiac steady alongside while Brent pulled first Tessa, then Sandra into the boat. They fell onto their knees in the bottom, and both men helped them out of their diving gear. "Thank God you're safe," Adam said, holding Sandra so tightly she cried out in pain.

"Sorry," he said, pulling away. He studied her, needing to reassure himself she was all right. "What the hell do you think you were doing, heading out on your own that way?" he demanded.

"I had to get this." She reached into the polypropylene bag at her side and took out a long, slender length of metal.

"What is it?" he asked, though he knew before she answered.

"It belonged to Passionata." She handed it to him. "It's broken, but I'm sure there's enough there to make a good identification."

He stared at the coiled serpent, whose body formed a grip and shield for the hand, and examined the one remaining ruby eye, which gleamed dully from the tarnished snake's head, and a chill rushed up his back. He grabbed a rag from the bottom of the dinghy and rubbed at the tarnish on the blade. Was that an inscription? Maybe. They'd have to wait until conservation to be sure.

"The wind's really picking up," Brent said. "We'd better get back to the ship."

"Right." He turned and fired up the motor once more, afraid to look at Sandra again, too much emotion crowding his throat and stinging his eyes.

Their arrival at the *Caspian* was greeted with shouts, but there wasn't much time for celebration, as they were almost immediately underway. "Why are we moving?" Sandra asked.

"Hurricane Larry is headed this way, and it's a big one," Charlie said.

"Expected to be a category five by the time it reaches here," Roger said. "No way we'd want to try to tough that out."

"We'll drop the two of you off near your yachts," Sam said. "You'll want to set sail as soon as possible."

Sandra turned to Adam. "I want to come with you," she said.

"What about your yacht?" he asked.

"My crew can take care of it. You'll need help with yours."

"I'd like to have you along." He cleared his throat. "We have a lot to talk about."

"Yes, we do," she agreed.

AFTER A BRIEF STOP at her yacht to collect some personal items and explain the plan to her crew, Sandra transferred to Adam's yacht and they prepared to set sail. They said little until they were underway. She was glad to be able to focus on the work of setting out to sea. Now that they were alone, she was having second thoughts about her impulsive decision to sail with Adam. Though he hadn't objected to her presence, he hadn't welcomed her with open arms, either.

She shrugged off her doubts. She wasn't the kind of woman to give up easily on what she wanted; fifteen years of scratching and clawing her way to the top of television news had proven that. She owed it to herself to learn if Adam loved her, and if so, what he intended to do about it.

When they were under sail, she made coffee and sandwiches in the yacht's compact galley and brought them to Adam at the wheel. "Thanks," he said, accepting a mug and a sandwich. "With this strong wind we should make good time to Jamaica and be safely in port before the storm hits."

"What did you do with the sword?" she asked.

"Cutlass. It's shorter and thicker than a sword," he corrected, and she almost smiled. He was ever the academic. "It's in one of the saline tanks on board the *Caspian*. Brent will look after it."

"You haven't asked me where I found it."

He leaned back against the wheel and sipped his coffee. "Where did you find it?" he asked.

"I found it on the missing section of the *Eve*."

He blinked. "The missing section?"

She nodded, amused by his attempt to remain cool and

unemotional. "It's resting on the ocean floor about a quarter mile southeast of the rest of the ship."

"Do you think you could find it again?" he asked.

She hesitated. "I don't know. Maybe. Tessa and I got turned around. We came to the surface to see if we could spot any landmarks. That's where you found us."

"How did you know where to look?" he asked.

"I had a dream," she said.

"A dream about Passionata?"

She took it as a good sign that there was no mocking in his voice. "In a way. At first I was swimming underwater, then I saw the wreck you found. Only it wasn't a wreck, but the ship as it must have looked at the time it sank. I swam farther and came across the stern. And then, I was on the ship, taking the sword—I mean, the cutlass—from its hiding place."

"You were Passionata."

She nodded. "I know it sounds crazy, but at the wreck site, when I held the cutlass in my hand, for a moment I was her again." She shivered and rubbed her arms, remembering. "I was standing on the deck of the *Eve,* the wind in my hair. It was so *real.* I felt like the most powerful woman in the world."

He nodded.

His silence unnerved her. "I'm not crazy," she said.

"I know you're not." He set aside his mug and plate and put his hands on her shoulders. "When I thought you were lost, I'm the one who felt I'd lost my mind," he said. "I realized how stupid I'd been, to let anything come between us."

"I don't blame you for not believing me," she said. "It is a wild story."

He squeezed her shoulders. "No wilder than a grown

man spending years searching for a ship that sank three hundred years ago. But I wonder now…maybe I was really searching for you."

A shiver chased up her back at his words. "Maybe you were," she said softly.

"Do you know how I found you?" he asked.

"No."

"I closed my eyes and concentrated on feeling you. On feeling that connection between us."

Her heart beat faster. "And you felt it?"

He nodded. "A picture came into my mind as clearly as if I was watching a movie. I saw you in the water, and I knew as long a I kept that picture clear in my mind, it would lead me right to you."

"So you think there is a connection between me and Passionata and you and Frederick?"

The lines at the corners of his eyes deepened. "I don't know about that. And I don't see any way to ever prove it. But I do believe there's a connection between the two of us. Something that goes beyond sexual attraction and common interests."

She smiled. "I think some people call that love."

He nodded. "I think they do. I love you, Sandra."

"I love you, too."

He pulled her into his arms and kissed her, and for a long moment neither spoke, lost in an embrace she prayed would never truly end. Forever they would be together and be invisibly linked.

At last they drew apart enough to catch their breath. Adam stroked the side of her face with the back of his fingers. "Do you think there's room in your life for a slightly rumpled professor who can be obsessive about his work?" he asked.

"If there's room in yours for a television journalist who can be pretty single-minded about her job." She kissed his palm. "Though that may be changing."

"Why is that?"

"This summer has made me think about a lot of things," she said. "I've fought so long and hard to stay on top, but in the end, I'm only as good as my last project. I'm tired of playing the game and bending over backward to please others. From now on, I want to work on projects of my own choosing, and complete them at my own pace. If the network doesn't want them, I'll find someone who does." All these thoughts had been tumbling in her head for weeks. Saying them aloud now felt empowering and absolutely right.

"So you'd form your own production company?" he asked.

"Something like that. What do you think?"

"I think it's a great idea." He grinned. "You know, I might have some money to invest soon. After the treasure we've salvaged is sold."

"Don't you want it for another expedition?"

"I'll use some of it for that, but it's always good to diversify. Especially if you're looking for a partner."

She shook her head. "I'm not looking anymore. I've found him."

He kissed her again, lightly on the lips. "Does this mean I'm forgiven, Passionata?"

"It does, Frederick."

Hurricane Causes Heavy Damage

Hurricane Larry cut a swath of destruction across the Caribbean last week as it barreled through the region with sustained winds of up to 170 miles per hour. An 18-foot storm surge knocked out power and is responsible for the death of three people on the tiny island of Nevis.

Passionata's Island, an uninhabited atoll owned by Great Britain, was completely wiped off the map by the storm, obliterated by the force of wind and water. Television personality Sandra Newman had been filming a documentary on the island and evacuated only hours before the storm hit. She and Professor Adam Carroway, a historian from the University of Michigan, arrived in Miami aboard the professor's yacht, the *Double Dare* Wednesday afternoon. Carroway had been leading a team that was excavating what is believed to be the wreck of the pirate ship the *Eve,* flagship of notorious female pirate Passionata, for whom the island was named.

"A hurricane of this magnitude causes great disturbances along the ocean floor, as well as at the surface," Carroway said at the press conference he'd called to announce his team's discovery of gold, silver and jewels, as well as a bronze-and-silver cutlass that belonged to Passionata. "I hope to return to the area next summer for further exploration, but the remains of the *Eve* may be like the island itself—lost to us forever."

* * * * *

Here's a sneak peek at THE CEO'S CHRISTMAS PROPOSITION, the first in USA TODAY *bestselling author Merline Lovelace's* HOLIDAYS ABROAD *trilogy coming in November 2008.*

American Devon McShay is about to get the Christmas surprise of a lifetime when she meets her new client, sexy billionaire Caleb Logan, for the very first time.

Silhouette
Desire

Available November 2008.

Her breath whistled out in a sigh of relief when he exited Customs. Devon recognized him right away from the newspaper and magazine articles her friend and partner Sabrina had looked up during her frantic prep work.

Caleb John Logan, Jr. Thirty-one. Six-two. With jet-black hair, laser-blue eyes and a linebacker's shoulders under his charcoal-gray cashmere overcoat. His jaw-dropping good looks didn't score him any points with Devon. She'd learned the hard way not to trust handsome heartbreakers like Cal Logan.

But he was a client. An important one. And she was willing to give someone who'd served a hitch in the marines before earning a B.S. from the University of Oregon, an MBA from Stanford and his first million at the ripe old age of twenty-six the benefit of the doubt.

Right up until he spotted the hot-pink pashmina, that is.

Devon knew the flash of color was more visible than the sign she held up with his name on it. So she wasn't surprised when Logan picked her out of the crowd and cut in her direction. She'd just plastered on her best business-woman smile when he whipped an arm around her waist.

The next moment she was sprawled against his cashmere-covered chest.

"Hello, brown eyes."

Swooping down, he covered her mouth with his.

Sheer astonishment kept Devon rooted to the spot for a few seconds while her mind whirled chaotically. Her first thought was that her client had downed a few too many drinks during the long flight. Her second, that he'd mistaken the kind of escort and consulting services her company provided. Her third shoved everything else out of her head.

The man could kiss!

His mouth moved over hers with a skill that ignited sparks at a half-dozen flash points throughout her body. Devon hadn't experienced that kind of spontaneous combustion in a while. A *long* while.

The sparks were still popping when she pushed off his chest, only now they fueled a flush of anger.

"Do you always greet women you don't know with a lip-lock, Mr. Logan?"

A smile crinkled the skin at the corners of his eyes. "As a matter of fact, I don't. That was from Don."

"Huh?"

"He said he owed you one from New Year's Eve two years ago and made me promise to deliver it."

She stared up at him in total incomprehension. Logan hooked a brow and attempted to prompt a nonexistent memory.

"He abandoned you at the Waldorf. Five minutes before midnight. To deliver twins."

"I don't have a clue who or what you're…"

Understanding burst like a water balloon.

"Wait a sec. Are you talking about Sabrina's old boyfriend? Your buddy, who's now an ob-gyn doc?"

It was Logan's turn to look startled. He recovered faster than Devon had, though. His smile widened into a rueful grin.

"I take it you're not Sabrina Russo."

"No, Mr. Logan, I am *not*."

* * * * *

Be sure to look for
THE CEO'S CHRISTMAS PROPOSITION
by Merline Lovelace.
Available in November 2008 wherever books are sold,
including most bookstores, supermarkets, drugstores and
discount stores.

REQUEST YOUR FREE BOOKS!

2 FREE NOVELS PLUS 2 FREE GIFTS!

HARLEQUIN®

Blaze™

Red-hot reads!

HARLEQUIN®

Blaze™

COMING NEXT MONTH

#429 KISS & TELL Alison Kent
In the world of celebrity tabloids, Caleb MacGregor is the best. Once he smells a scandal, he makes sure the world knows. And that's exactly what Miranda Kelly is afraid of. Hiding behind her stage name, Miranda hopes she'll avoid his notice. And she does—until she invites Caleb into her bed.

#430 UNLEASHED Lori Borrill
It's a wild ride in more ways than one when Jessica Beane is corralled into a road trip by homicide detective Rick Marshall. Crucial evidence is missing and Jess is the key to unlocking not just the case, but their pent-up passion, as well!

#431 A BODY TO DIE FOR Kimberly Raye
Love at First Bite, Bk. 3
Vampire Viviana Darland is in Skull Creek, Texas, looking for one thing—an orgasm. Or more specifically, the only man who's ever given her one, vampire Garret Sawyer. She knows her end is near, and wants one good climax before she goes. And she intends to get it—before Garret delivers on his promise to kill her....

#432 HER SEXIEST SURPRISE Dawn Atkins
He's the best birthday gift ever! When Chloe Baxter makes a sexy wish on her birthday candles, she never expects Riley Connelly—her secret crush—to appear. Nor does she expect him to give her the hottest night of her life. It's so hot, why share just one night?

#433 RECKLESS Tori Carrington
Indecent Proposals, Bk. 1
Heidi Joblowski isn't a woman to leave her life to chance. Her plan? To marry her perfect boyfriend, Jesse, and have several perfect children. Unfortunately, the only perfect thing in her life lately is the sex she's been having with Jesse's best friend Kyle....

#434 IN A BIND Stephanie Bond
Sex for Beginners, Bk. 2
Flight attendant Zoe Smythe is working her last shift, planning her wedding... and doing her best to ignore the sexual chemistry between her and a seriously sexy Australian passenger. But when she reads a letter she'd written in college, reminding her of her most private, erotic fantasies...all bets are off!

www.eHarlequin.com